11-07

Outlaw
Princess
of Sherwood

Outlaw Princess
of Sherwood

A TALE OF ROWAN HOOD

NANCY SPRINGER

PHILOMEL BOOKS ⚜ NEW YORK

Published simultaneously in Canada. Printed in the United States of America.
Design by Gunta Alexander. The text is set in Apollo.

Library of Congress Cataloging-in-Publication Data
Springer, Nancy. Outlaw princess of Sherwood, a tale of Rowan Hood / Nancy Springer.
p. cm. Sequel to: Lionclaw, a tale of Rowan Hood.
Summary: King Solon the Red attempts to capture his runaway daughter Ettarde and force her
into marriage with a rival king who has been threatening his reign.
[1. Kings, queens, rulers, etc.—Fiction. 2. Princesses—Fiction. 3. Fathers and daughters—
Fiction. 4. Robin Hood (Legendary character)—Fiction.] I. Title. PZ7.S76846Ot 2003
[Fic]—dc21   2003000075   ISBN 0-399-23721-6
1   3   5   7   9   10   8   6   4   2
First Impression

To Jaime

One

Danger! Etty thought, or sensed, stiffening. She listened one instant longer, and yes, that muffled sound was the clop of hooves on forest loam. *Horsemen!*

She ran. Gathering her apron full of cresses, she sprinted toward the tall oaks of Sherwood Forest. Lady have mercy, forest stood everywhere, yet there she was, caught in the middle of Fountain Dale, in the open, and it sounded like many hooves, many riders, very near. The spring rains had soaked the Nottingham Way, and the softened ground had not given her much warning.

Nor would the forest offer much safety, for only birches and alders were yet in leaf. But the hazel bushes edging the meadow grew thick enough to hide behind.

Darting for cover, Etty gave the hissing call of the wryneck bird to signal Rowan in the quietest way she could. But Rowan already knew. Out of the corner of one eye Etty saw Rowan, daughter of Robin Hood, lifting her green kirtle, her brown braid lashing like a wildcat's tail as she tried to run. Rowan's broken legs had healed over the winter, but were not yet strong.

She fell.

With a gasp, Etty saw Rowan sprawl headlong on the spring-green meadow. From just beyond the first bend of the Nottingham Way came the sounds of harness jingling and creaking, the rough voices of laughing men.

Letting go of her apron, letting cresses strew the grass, Etty dashed toward Rowan, bad memories flashing through her mind, as always when something went wrong. *The man trap.* As if it were happening right now Etty could hear the horrible jaws clashing shut on Rowan's legs, could hear her scream, could hear the snap of her breaking bones . . . And when the foresters had come, like an idiot Etty had cried out Rowan's name, then run away.

Lionel, Rook, Robin Hood, Rowan herself, they had all said Etty had just showed good sense, running away, for what could she have done against two armed men? But Etty knew better. She knew she had lost her head.

She knew herself to be a coward.

Even now, running toward Rowan, she felt the panic

again and knew herself unworthy to wear the silver ring, emblem of the Rowan Hood band, the single strand that shone on her right hand.

Rowan was struggling to heave herself up from the ground, as if she'd had the breath knocked out of her. She had only clambered to her hands and knees when Etty reached her, grabbed her under the shoulders and lifted her, almost carrying her. With all her strength Etty heaved Rowan through a gap in the hazel bushes. Behind the thick, sheltering roots they collapsed together.

"Thank you," Rowan gasped, still panting for breath.

"Shhh." Etty wanted no thanks.

Rowan panted, "Toads take it . . . I wasn't expecting . . . a cavalcade. . . ."

"Hush."

Flat on the ground behind the bushes, huddled into dead weeds and keeping their heads down, they both hushed as the horsemen clattered into the meadow.

"Halt!" roared a man's voice less than ten paces away, and there was sudden silence, broken only by the snorting and pawing of horses and the scolding of the jaybirds in the oaks.

In that silence Etty could hear her own heart thumping in her ears, its pounding beat seeming to say No—

no—no. No, it could not be. It was just her craven heart making her imagine that she knew that voice.

"What say you, sirrah?" the same voice demanded. "You deem this is the place?"

Another man's tame tones replied, "Yes, Your Highness."

Etty bit her lip to keep from crying out. She felt Rowan's hand close over hers, warm, steadying. One careless move and all would be over.

"Are you certain?" barked the harsh voice of Solon the Red, petty king of Auberon. Etty's father.

"Yes, Your Highness. It was here. There is the fountain and all."

"Hah. Assuming the wench is still hereabouts, then, we'll have her at our mercy."

Wench. He meant her, his daughter, Ettarde.

He had come to reclaim her.

Etty started to tremble. She had not yet dared a look at her father, but just at the sound of his voice she felt herself once again Ettarde of Auberon, runaway princess, damsel in distress. For that moment she forgot that she was now Etty, member of an outlaw band. She shook like a frightened deer. All her muscles bunched, and against all reason she felt sure that her angry father could see her; right through the hazel bushes and her

4

brown mantle with its hood shadowing her face he could still see her. She knew that she must be motionless, still and silent like a big-eared mouse in its bed of leaves, or else she would be seen and captured—yet her heart raced, urging her to leap up and run, fly, flee, run away, run away.

"To your stations!" King Solon roared. "Pitch camp!"

The shock of his shout made Etty startle all over. If it were not for men leaping from their horses, someone might have heard the brush rattle. Rowan's warm hand slipped up to Etty's wrist, gripping her.

It was not only her own life that depended on silence. It was Rowan's also.

Yet in the back of her mind panic babbled, *Run! Go ahead, be a coward. Run away!*

Running had worked to her advantage once before. Almost a year ago. An evening in early summer, here, at this very spot, when she had still been a sorrowing princess dressed in white satin and lace, with her father's men escorting her to be married to Lord Basil against her will. All had been the noise and confusion of men making camp, just as it was now. With her head nestled at the base of the hazel bush Ettarde could hear them yelling orders at each other, quarreling, leading horses here and there. At just such a time last summer she had taken her chance and had run into the shadows of the forest.

But they would have caught her at once if Rowan had not been there to help her. And Lionel, great oaf of a minstrel who would tremble at the sight of a spider—yet he had faced an armored knight to save her.

Head down behind the hazel bush, Etty listened to the commotion in Fountain Dale and watched Rowan's grave, dark-eyed face. She signaled Rowan with lifted eyebrows and a pleading gaze: *Now? Please?*

By way of answer, Rowan increased the warm pressure of her grip on Etty's wrist: *Wait.* But at the same time, Rowan lifted her head softly, ever so slowly—Rowan had her father's knack of moving as silently as a spirit in the woods. Etty watched as Rowan edged over and peeked between the hazels. She saw Rowan's face go stark.

Only the sight of evil gave Rowan that look.

Something evil.

But no immediate danger. Rowan had not moved. With her heart pounding painfully, Etty eased her own head up until she could catch a glimpse of her father's encampment through the bushes.

At first she could make little sense of the bits and pieces she saw between hazel stems. Lances with their butts set into the ground, their pennons bearing her father's device: a white rose on a red ground. Horses, bay and dapple gray. Men-at-arms in plumed helmets and red quilted tabards with the white rose riding like a breastplate on their chests. A wagon decked in white and red—the very wagon that had carried her, an unwilling bride under guard, to this spot. Hazily Etty wondered why they had brought the wagon along; perhaps it was meant to carry her onward to Lord Basil now? How arrogant of her father to assume he would capture her. There he towered, King Solon of Auberon, still on his blood-bay steed as if on a tall, living throne, his red beard waxed into a precise point like a logic problem, his hard-nailed finger pointing as he directed his men. Even in her hiding place, Etty seemed to feel that finger stab her like a spear to the heart, seemed to feel the glare of his flinty eyes under brows waxed into red wings. Feeling as weak as if she were kneeling at his feet, it took her a moment to realize what project he was overseeing, what evil thing his men were erecting.

Lady have mercy.

A cage.

It stood in the very center of Fountain Dale, at the heart of the meadow, halfway between the forest and the spring that gave the place its name. Ten feet tall, it looked like a toy mistakenly left there by a giant. At Auberon there had been linnets and nightingales kept in cages in the solarium, pretty cages with golden bars aspiring from a circular base to meet gracefully at the top. This cage was like those, graceful and golden, but meant for some far larger songbird.

Meant for me.

At first Etty could hardly bear the thought, but then she felt anger start to burn like a dragon in her chest. If her father thought he was going to put her in that cage, he could think again. Not a moment longer would she sit still for his tyranny. Ettarde tugged against Rowan's hand. *Let's go! Please?*

But Rowan did not respond. Rowan lay there like an outlaw girl carved of wood. And in a moment Etty saw why. As the men stepped back, their work completed, she saw that the cage was not meant for her after all. Or not exactly. With a shock to the heart of her heart, Etty saw that there was already someone in it.

A woman.

A lady, rather. Delicate. Slender.

Barefoot. And bare-legged, wearing only a muslin chemise ripped off at her knees. Hugging her own bare shoulders in the springtime chill. Shivering.

Long hair the color of tarnished silver flowing down her back.

A perfect, pale, symmetrical face much like Ettarde's own.

Still mouth. Shadowed eyes.

At her first glimpse, Etty felt her whole body clench around the sudden yearning pain in her heart. She wanted to cry out like a baby.

My mother.

Two

N o fire," Rowan ordered.

"But my dear Rowan," complained Lionel, "they won't see it. There's rock all around." The Rowan Hood band sat within a cup of massive stone, sheltered by an encircling grove.

Etty listened as the others within the rowan hollow talked, but she could not speak, could not react.

"They might see the smoke," said Rowan. She was right. Fountain Dale lay not much more than a furlong away.

"But it's twilight! They won't see smoke at night!"

"Then they'll see the glow on the crags. No fire."

Etty felt as if she were watching and listening from a great distance. Even though she huddled shoulder to shoulder with the others around a sweetwater spring that had not failed all winter, even here, with her friends, she felt alone. Shock hazed her like mist that would not rise, clung to her like the odor of swamp water.

"No fire, no supper," said Lionel, pouting his baby-ish mouth, widening his baby blue eyes to look pathetic. "And what if I starve to death before morning?" Like his gigantic height, Lionel's prodigious appetite was a joke among them. By his soft sideward glance, Etty knew he was trying to make her smile, but she couldn't.

"Cold venison," Rowan said.

"And not even cresses to go with it."

"Poor wee laddie. No, no cresses. And no singing, either." Rowan gave Lionel a severe look with laughter hidden behind it. "Yet somehow you *will* survive."

Always the members of the Rowan Hood band joked among themselves, no matter how hard times were—and times had been very hard this past winter. They had joked about not being able to wash without perishing of cold. That had been harder than hunger for Etty, not being able to keep herself clean and dainty, but the others had helped her bear it. They had joked about the fleas and lice that feasted upon their dirty bodies. They had joked about hunger and cold. Joking warmed the cold and defied the rain.

Or, in this case, the reign of King Solon the Red, too close at hand.

Rowan added, "They will be sending out scouts. We must take care. No one is to go anywhere alone."

"Especially not Etty," said Lionel, not joking any longer as he turned to Ettarde. "My dear lady, don't even walk into the brush by yourself."

Any other time she would have grumbled at him, "I'm not your dear lady!" Or she would have told him she could relieve herself without his comment or assistance, thank you. But she felt too fogged to reply.

Rowan said, "The whole time we were hiding behind that hazel bush, I was dreading that one of them might come over and pee on us."

Laughter. But Etty could not laugh.

"Shhh!" With a visible effort Rowan quieted. "We have to think." Her glance caught on the wolf-dog who lay panting and grinning atop the boulders, and she focused on him with rueful affection. "I don't know what to do about Tykell," she said, mostly to herself. "On the one hand, when he's around, he is our best guard. He can provide Etty with an escort that will not offend her delicacy." Rowan smiled, but once again Etty could not answer her smile. Rowan continued, "But on the other hand, when he's wandering, he may venture to Fountain Dale. . . ."

Rook spoke up. "The forest is vast. We should move."

At the sound of the wild boy's low, gruff voice,

everyone turned. Even Tykell ceased his panting to listen. Rook spoke seldom, always briefly, and often with wisdom. Leave the rowan hollow. Move to somewhere else in Sherwood Forest. Leave Fountain Dale far behind until the danger was past. Yes.

No. Violently Etty shook her head. Her sight blurred. She heard Rowan say, "Etty?"

She hid her face in her hands, longing for the relief of tears, but her eyes felt like hot stones; she could not cry.

As if sensing the presence of a warm ghost, she felt Rowan kneel in front of her. As lightly as doves, Rowan's hands settled one on each side of Etty's head, nesting there like—like a blessing. Rowan, with the blood of *aelfe*, forest spirits, in her veins—even her touch had a healing power.

Etty felt strengthened enough to lift her head and sob. "My mother! He's put my mother in a cage!" Tears stung her eyes. She had not expected ever to see her gentle lady mother again. Such a reunion should have been the happiest of miracles. But no, her father had to have his wrongheaded way. So now this.

Without moving her hands from Etty's head, her grave face only inches away, Rowan said, "I know."

"He's making her suffer to bait me!"

"Shhh. Keep your voice down. They'll hear you."

Etty lowered her voice only slightly. "I don't care what they do. We have to save her."

Rook said, "No. We have to save *you*."

Etty jerked her head away from Rowan's touch to turn and glare at Rook. Hot and black, like coals, his eyes glittered back at her from under his shaggy black hair.

Woods colt, she wanted to snap at him, do you even *have* a mother? But Etty's mother had trained her to be a princess, calm and sweet and always in control of herself, behaving with ladylike decorum no matter what. Not very practical rules for an outlaw girl . . . yet, thinking of her mother, Etty forced herself to speak softly. "You cannot save me by making me betray my first loyalty."

"Your first loyalty should be to the band," Rook said.

"No." Rowan gentled Etty's hair again. "We love our mothers first, Rook. Even Robin would tell you the same, I think." Rowan settled back into her place against the stones.

Lionel said, "Ettarde." He spoke like the lord's son he was. Etty turned to him.

Lionel said quietly, "Etty, your mother is being humiliated, I know, but how is she in need of rescue? She is not being harmed."

Cabbagehead, Etty thought, taking a deep breath to

keep from shouting at him. Between clenched teeth she said, "Can't you see that she is out in the cold in only her shift—"

"I have not seen her at all."

He truly did not understand? "Well, she is."

"We don't know that. Perhaps he has taken her in now."

"You don't know my father," Etty said.

"True."

"He will leave her out there and he will starve her." Etty remembered what her father had done to her, his daughter and his only living child, after he had arranged for her to marry Lord Basil but she had refused. He had locked her up to starve also. Not in a cage. He had imprisoned her in her tower chamber with its canopied goosedown bed, tree-of-Eden tapestries, her window paned with real glass and by the window her chair carved all over with griffins, and her linens and embroidery flosses and—and her little shelf of books; that was the only memory that gave Ettarde a pang of longing. Her library bound in tooled and gilded kidskin: Marcus Aurelius, Plutarch, Ovid, Virgil, Homer, Pliny, Herodotus, Plato, and more. Starving in her chamber, she had taken comfort in reading the philosophers—at first. Later she had not been able to read for thinking of food.

By the tenth day, her clothes had started to hang loose on her and hunger had driven her almost out of her mind. That day, after her serving women had dressed her, she had stripped off her satin-and-velvet gown in a fury. She had flung her necklace of gold and garnets against the wall. She had seized the rosewood casket in which she kept her jewelry—gold and silver, amber, emeralds, chalcedony—and dumped it all on the floor, stamping on the jewels because she could not eat them.

Dressed only in her chemise. As her mother was now.

"He will not give her a blanket," Etty said. "The night is cold." With a harsh, hurtful desire she wanted to take warmth, food, love to her mother. Even though she herself sat on stone, amid shadows of nightfall, under stark trees, she wished this. But she knew that her father's men lay in wait to seize her.

With little hope of any help, only talking her way through her own misery, Etty said, "He will give her bread and water, perhaps. To keep her alive until he captures me."

"You know him," Lionel said. "How long will he starve her? He will give it up eventually, won't he?"

With no more tone than stones dropping, Rook said, "We should leave."

"Till he sees it's no use," Lionel added more gently.

Etty clenched her fists, eyes blurring till she could barely see Lionel's big full-moon face. "And if it were *your* mother?" she cried at him.

Silence. Somewhere amid the oaks and crags, a fox whimpered. As if the forest itself had sighed, a breath of air stirred, smelling of wet loam and mushrooms. Through bare branches, stars winked like imp eyes. Etty shivered, wrapping her old brown mantle more tightly around herself. Feeling her nose running, she reached for the kerchief tucked in her sleeve. Her hand felt scratchy against her arm, callused from bow and arrow, roughened from gathering firewood, digging roots, shelling walnuts. She had not been able to spare her hands, but at least she still used a kerchief. Just because she was an outlaw didn't mean she had to wipe her nose on her sleeve, like Rowan, or let her hair grow all knotted and clotted like Rook's. She had managed to keep the golden-brown sheen in her hair, her face clean and its skin petal-soft and smooth, the way her mother had taught her.

Mother . . .

"If it were my mother," came Lionel's soft reply, "I'd feel as you do, of course. But . . ."

But feeling was no use, he meant, though he was too gentle to say it. Or feeling for the caged lady was all very well, but there was no way to save her.

Rowan sighed like the forest, then said, "Etty, I'll go tomorrow and speak with Robin. Maybe . . . I don't know. Maybe he'll be able to think of some way to help. Just please, promise you won't do anything tonight."

Etty kept her promise—more or less. It was dawn before she slipped away.

Three

Etty had not been able to eat or sleep. She had spent the night with her eyes burning and blinking, with her empty belly aching like her overfull heart. Even wrapped in her mantle plus two blankets, she had shivered with cold. Partly it was an inner cold that blankets could not warm, yet she lay all too aware of how frost stiffened her hair, furred her blankets. Had Father allowed Mother a blanket against the frost?

In her heart, Etty knew better.

By the time the morning star rose, chilly and brilliant like her father's mind, she could not bear to lie there any longer. Rising at first light, her breath hanging white in the air, Etty pulled on stagskin boots, then slipped out of the rowan hollow and away toward Fountain Dale.

Her boots left a plain trail in the frost. Etty did not care, for being in motion eased her heartache somewhat.

She wanted to run, leap, fly to her mother, but she made herself walk slowly, silently, drifting like a deer between the white-fingered rowans and oaks and blackthorn. She would decide when she saw her mother whether to give herself up. Until then, she would be an outlaw a little while longer.

Noiselessly she made her way along the ridge, where the day's first watery sunshine touched the stones, melting the frost so that it soaked her skirt and boots worse than dew. When she judged that the clearing lay below, she began to edge her way down the wet, rocky slope. Sunlight trickled through bare branches onto fern fiddleheads and green spears of wake-robin pushing up through last year's leaves. And coltsfoot. In the poor stony soil between rocks bloomed the first flower of spring. Looking down at the shaggy little plant with its hoof-shaped leaves and yellow sunburst blossoms, Etty remembered that Rowan had strewn coltsfoot on her mother's body.

It had been exactly a year since Rowan's mother had been killed.

All that talk of mothers last night, yet Rowan had not said a word of her own mother, the half-*aelfin* healer put to death by the lord's henchmen.

The thought hushed Etty's crying heart as she

ghosted downslope between rifts of stone and holly and hemlock to the rich valley where mighty oaks grew. Morning lay silver and still on the forest. The oaks, their buds just blooming into tassel, hung silent. Etty heard no sound except the sleepy twittering of sparrows, and her own breath, no longer white; the day was warming slightly. As she slipped between giant, mossy tree trunks, her feet made no sound on loam and wet layers of old leaves. She began to hurry her steps, for there, ahead, rising above the hazel thickets she could see the cage.

And there, far closer, standing against the trunk of an oak, a guard.

He stood in full view, facing her. He had to see her. Etty's breath stopped and she froze like a hare, her heart pounding fit to split her chest open. A full stricken moment passed before she realized he was asleep on his feet, at attention with his eyes closed. He would be flogged if he were caught.

Breathing again, taking one slow step at a time, Etty inched behind the nearest tree and pressed against its rough bark until her thudding heart quieted and she could think what to do next.

She knew she should steal away. But she couldn't. Her mother . . .

And guards set by her father, who expected her to do just what she was doing. Not all the guards would be asleep.

She listened. Looked around her. Then gathered her skirt and moved, creeping her way on hands and knees toward the hazels. *Please*, in her mind she prayed to the wise and ancient spirits of hazel as Rowan had taught her, *please shelter me, please let me not be seen.*

She wormed her way deep into a copse of hazels, wincing when a branch rustled—but no cry was raised. Lying flat on cold, sodden ground between the roots, Etty breathed hard for a moment before easing her head up to look.

There. Mother.

Queen Elsinor of Auberon. And before her marriage, Lady Elsinor of Celydon. Had Mother ever gone a day of her life till now without a silk petticoat and a velvet gown and slippers of softest kidskin for her feet?

Hunched in the middle of the bare cage, Etty's mother hugged her bare knees with her bare arms, her bare feet huddled together like puppies, blue with cold. The sight squeezed Etty's heart like an iron fist. It was as she had expected: Her father had allowed her mother no blanket for covering against the frosty night.

Looking upon what her father had done, Etty felt herself burn like iron in a forge. With white heat she hated, hated, hated, hated her father, hated him more for her mother's sake than she had ever hated him before. When he had starved her, Ettarde, it had been because she had defied him. But what had Mother ever done but bear his children and bow to his slightest whim?

From her hiding place, Etty could see heads through the bars of the cage. Four guards surrounded it, north and south and east and west. Three of the heads nodded, either sleepy or dozing. And the guard who stood closest to Etty was clearly asleep, leaning on his spear to drowse.

Etty felt all of her muscles bunching like a cat readying itself to spring. She would run to her mother, thrust her mantle into the cage and run away again before the guards could rouse enough to catch her. No, confusion take it all, they *would* catch her, but it didn't matter, if they would let Mother out of the cage and put her in it instead. Confound her father, devil shave his pointed beard, blast everything, he could do to her what he liked. Nothing mattered except helping Mother.

In the cage, Queen Elsinor lifted her head suddenly, her tarnished-silver tresses stirring on her thin back. She looked at the sleeping guard. She scanned the edge of the clearing with shadowed eyes. Then in a voice as clear and trembling as a dewdrop, she began to sing.

"All you ladies gentle and fair,
Come take warning from my plight.
The man I wed has left me here
Caged and shivering in the night."

In the dawn hush, her voice fluted like the call of a mistle thrush. The guards straightened, turned their heads, peered at her. Etty sank back to the ground and swallowed tears, remembering her mother's silver voice singing her a lullaby when she was little, her mother's slender hands tucking the blankets more firmly around her chin. This melody she remembered well, but never before had her mother sung to her these words.

When Etty looked again, her mother stood like a lonesome spirit in the cage. In the chill dawn, Queen Elsinor sang on:

"All you maidens, hear me sing,
Let no man put you in a cage.
Little songbirds, take to the wing
and fly, fly—"

"Stop it!" roared a voice Etty knew all too well. Out of the largest tent burst her father, his boots unlaced, his tunic awry, his beard pointing in all directions like a thornbush. Etty stared, for she had never before seen him in such disarray.

From the cage Mother sang, "Fly, fly far away—"

"Shut your mouth!" King Solon the Red strode to the cage with menace in his shoulders. Not that he would strike her. But a blow would have been kinder than what he was doing to her.

"My singing displeases you, good my majesty?" inquired Etty's mother with the greatest ladylike courtesy. Because the floor of the cage raised her, she stood taller than he did.

"None of your games," he told her, as grim as a black-hooded executioner.

"Games? But my lord and master, I remember when you loved to hear my voice lifted in song."

Etty felt her mouth open in soundless wonder. There had once been love between her mother and her father, then? She had never thought to ask, had always assumed her mother had been married off to her father for the sake of a political alliance, in just such an arranged wedlock as Father had tried to force upon her, Ettarde. After all, Mother had been only a girl of sixteen. But— had Father courted her, then?

Apparently so. And even the empty memory of love seemed to give Mother heart. Facing the angry king of

Auberon, Queen Elsinor shivered no longer. She smiled down on him as if she were receiving a garland of roses from his hand.

"Bah!" The sound exploded from Etty's father like a curse. He raised his clenched fist. "No more, I tell you, or I will have them bind your mouth." He turned his back on her and stormed away, back to his tent.

Queen Elsinor stood as encaged as before. Yet somehow, Etty sensed, her mother had won.

Four

Etty blew her mother a kiss, then set her jaw and started worming her way out of the hazel bushes and back through the forest to the safety of the rowan grove.

The trumpeter had blown his bugle for morning, and King Solon's encampment seethed like an anthill now with sleepy men-at-arms stumbling out of tents, getting campfires started, tending horses, going out to relieve the sentries. Flat on her belly behind the first big oak she reached, lifting her head above its roots to watch guards take their positions, Etty began to feel safer. She knew where the relief sentries were positioned, and a little bit of brush rustling would not be heard amid the morning hubbub. She rose to her feet.

"I have her!" barked a man's voice.

It struck like a thunderbolt out of the clear sunrise

sky. Etty gasped and turned. There by a great elm stood a man-at-arms with his bow drawn and his honed steel arrowhead leveled at her.

"Don't move," he told her. He lifted his voice. "I have the princess, I say!" Answering shouts sounded from the camp.

In that same thunderbolt moment, before Etty could think beyond fear, there sounded a meaty *thwok*. Etty saw first the man's surprised face, then the feathered shaft jutting from his chest as he folded to the earth.

Her feet moved far more quickly than her thoughts. Yanking her skirt above her knees, she ran like a deer up the rocky slope toward the ridge.

Where had that arrow come from? She had never even seen it fly.

It had been a clothyard shaft fletched with gray goose feathers. It must have been shot by one of Robin Hood's men. Yet she saw no one.

From the valley behind her sounded shouts. "He's dead!"

"He said he had her and now—"

"She killed him!"

"Not *her*, lardhead! Look at the length of that shaft!"

"Outlaws!"

"This forest is crawling with—"

And then came her father's roar. "Fan out, cowards! We know she's close at hand! Find her!"

Sprinting as fast as she had ever run in her life, almost noiseless in her soft stagskin boots, Etty plunged over the ridge. Then her mind began to take charge, and she veered away from the rowan grove. Let them chase her all they wanted; she would not lead them back to the rowan grove and the others.

Her breath rasped in her throat, burned in her lungs. Her heart pounded. Her pulse roared in her ears. Panic roared in her mind, a lion, a crying baby, panic too much like the fear she had felt that other time she had run from her father. Rowan and Lionel had rescued her then. But she was going to have to fend for herself now.

The *crack!* of a breaking branch jolted Etty like a blow, sent her leaping forward. *Snap, crash,* close behind her men blundered through brush. Deep voices cursed.

Too close. In a moment they would spot her and be after her like hounds. And panting, with her ribs aching, Etty realized she could not run much farther. Wildly she scanned the trees, but they could not help her. Not enough leaves yet to conceal her if she climbed. If her father's men-at-arms had the sense to look up, they would see her. But she had to find somewhere to hide!

Like a hunted fox, she must go to ground. Too late she realized she should have headed for the crags after all, for there were many hiding places among the rocks. Here in the belly of Sherwood Forest there were only trees—

And fallen trees. Deadfalls everywhere.

There was not much time. Slowing to a lope, Etty looked around her, silently begging the forest, *Lady mother of us all, please, help me . . .* And there, at a small distance she spotted a likely deadfall screened by bracken. It had once been a mighty oak, its girth more than great enough to hide a skinny girl. Etty darted to the rotting oak, in pieces now, and crouched by the largest section of trunk to heave one side of it off the ground. Yes. Yes, Lady be praised, rot had hollowed it to a half shell. Straining to hold the heavy thing up a moment longer, Etty flopped on her side and squirmed underneath it. The log gave her just barely enough time to lie in its hollow before it fell back where it had been, covering her. Only then she thought to pray, *Sweet woods Lady, please, for the love of mercy, no snakes.*

It was so dark under there that a viper could have coiled by her nose and she wouldn't have known. The rotting wood pressed against her back, flattening her against sodden loam and perhaps worms, grubs, spiders . . . Etty tried to stop thinking about what might be under there with her. She tried to quiet her own breathing. The bracken would rustle if anyone came very near, but she had to be able to hear—

"I swear I heard someone up here!" shouted a man's voice near at hand.

Etty stiffened, breaking into a sudden sweat. Had she left tracks? Did the bracken show where she had run through? Was the skirt of her kirtle sticking out from under the log?

"Bah," said another man's voice. "She could be any-where."

"We'll be feeling King Solon's wrath unless we find her."

"I don't care. You saw what happened to Brock. I don't fancy an arrow in my gut."

Their voices moved away. Etty lay in the dirt, listening with her whole body and wishing it were over.

Rowan said, "You broke your promise. And you went there by yourself."

Etty said, "I know." Rowan did not sound angry, just worried. It might have been easier to face her if she had been angry.

"None of us got killed," Lionel grumbled to Rowan. "Let bad enough alone."

Nightfall hid the rowan hollow at the end of a long

day, and all of them sheltered there, Rowan and Lionel, Rook and Etty. With loam all over her kirtle and wood rot in her hair, Etty had seldom felt so dirty, but dirt was a small price to pay for her foolishness. Lady be praised that no one had captured her. Rowan and the others had been alerted by one of Robin's outlaws, none of them had come to harm, and now they all huddled together in the hollow. Tykell was off hunting somewhere. Lionel seemed even more peevish than usual, probably because he missed the pleasure of his harp and the warmth of a fire. But they were all alive, with bread and cheese and raw eggs to eat. It was over.

Till tomorrow.

Rowan said, "It's not ended yet. Ettarde, I need to know: Can I trust you?"

"I think so." Etty felt dead tired and not very sure of herself, but one thing she knew. "The song my mother sang was a signal to me," she said. "She wants me to stay away and be safe. And free. I never knew . . ." The memory of her mother's courage tightened her throat, and she could not speak.

"Never knew what?" Rowan put the question gently enough.

"Never knew she could be so brave."

"In my experience," Rowan said quietly, "a mother will do almost anything to save her child."

Etty could see Rowan's grave face only faintly, yet knew Rowan was remembering how her own mother, facing the lord's men as they set fire to the thatch over her head, had used her last strength sending a spell to protect Rowan.

Of her own mother Etty remembered no such courage—until now. Mostly she remembered her mother's caution. Mother teaching her how to gauge her father's mood and avoid his wrath. And compliance. Mother's voice outside her chamber door when she was locked up, whispering, "Dear heart, it's no use. Just do what he says." And one covert rebellion. Mother trying to bribe the guards with jewels. Trying to slip Ettarde something besides bread and water to eat.

That was probably what Father was feeding Mother. Bread and water. With the aroma of roasting meat rising from the soldiers' cooking fires all around.

"She sensed somehow that I might be there," Etty said, "and she woke the guards to keep me from doing anything stupid. She sang a song that told me to fly away."

Rowan regarded her with a softened look. Lionel reached for more bread and cheese. The rocks all around the rowan hollow lustered like tarnished silver in moonlight and starlight. Somewhere back in the thorny crags an owl mourned.

Rook said, "Then you should fly away."

Etty shook her head. Quietly enough she said, "No. I can't."

"But she wants you to."

"I can't let him treat her like—"

But her voice broke into a gasp, for a black head with no face popped up from behind the wall of rock, far too near her. Etty nearly screamed. Only remembering that they might hear her in Fountain Dale kept her from shrieking. She cringed, groping for the dagger stuck in her belt, gawking at the dark thing looming. It looked as if it could be a black-masked doomster ready to behead someone with an ax, or Guy of Gisborn in his black horsehide armor, or—or something worse, a specter out of the night.

Rook crouched and growled almost like the wolf-dog, Tykell. Lionel and Rowan leapt to their feet, snatching for weapons, their faces pale, shocked to their bones because they had been taken so badly by surprise. How had the intruder gotten so close without being heard?

In a high, creaky voice it spoke. "A morsel of bread, young gentry, or a taste of cheese? Will ye take pity on a poor wayfaring stranger?"

Dagger in hand, Etty felt her fear flare into annoyance. It was one of those accursed Wanderers, face hidden under the shadow of a black cowl. Stinking thing, it had no business being here. Its presence seemed to foul the hollow. Wanderers were filthy thieves, and how dare they beg when everyone knew they hid pouches full of gold and jewels under their black robes? Hard to tell from the voice whether this one was a man or a woman, but it scarcely mattered. Dirty, lying sneaks, they were all the same.

"Even just the crust of the bread?" it wheedled, face still hidden in the shadow of its black hood. "The hard rind of the cheese?"

Etty glanced at the others. Lionel's face showed distaste such as she herself felt, and he lowered his quarterstaff. Rook had stopped growling. But Rowan kept her bow at the ready, standing arrow-straight, staring intently at the black form just beyond the rocks. "How did you know we were here?" she challenged.

"They crawl everywhere," Lionel grumped, "like lice, or fleas."

"Hush," she told him without turning her gaze away from the intruder. "You, answer me. We showed no fire. How did you find us?" Her level gaze grew steely. Tall in her archer's stance, she drew the peacock-feathered butt of her flint-tipped arrow back to her ear.

Any sane person would have ducked behind the rocks, but the Wanderer froze where it was. It began to squeak and gibber with fear. "Mercy, young mistress! Mercy on a poor old, ah, old ah-ahh-ahhhh-choo!"

The force of the sneeze shot his head partway out of the hood. Etty caught a glimpse of something that gleamed in the moonlight. Surprise took her breath away.

Curly golden hair.

"Robin!" she squeaked.

"Oh, for the love of toads . . ." Rowan lowered her bow.

"Robin, you rascal, you . . ." Etty could not think of anything stinging enough to call him. She grabbed a pebble and flung it at him.

"Oww," he drawled in his own tenor voice, grinning, then coughing. He wiped his nose on his sleeve.

"*Father*," said Rowan, "what if I had shot you?"

"I knew you wouldn't." Flinging the hood back from his handsome face, Robin stood up and vaulted over the rocks, into the rowan hollow. Rowan gave him a kiss of greeting on his cheek, but Etty was in no mood to kiss him.

"What if one of us had screamed?" Rowan was still trying to chide her father.

"I knew you wouldn't."

"I nearly did," Etty complained. Even in moonlight she could see the glint of fun in his blue eyes. Blast the scamp, she had thought she was beyond being fooled by his pranks. If Tykell had been here, he would have wagged his tail, and Robin would have been discovered at once. Or if he had stood up, they would have known it was him, he was so tall. Or if—

"Don't you ever wash your face?" Robin asked gravely, peering at Etty. "It looks dark."

He was teasing her. And it would have taken a hard heart to resist the mischief dancing in his eyes. Etty had to smile.

"Here, Lionel, a snack for you." Robin pulled a large packet of something from under his mantle and tossed it to him. Pulling off its coarse cloth wrapping, Lionel released the sumptuous aroma of roast venison.

"Thanks!" he exclaimed, although of course it was not just for him. They all sat down to share it.

"No thanks called for." Robin coughed again. His voice sounded as clogged as his nose. Looking weary now, sitting within the hollow, he leaned against the rock.

"I owe thanks also," Etty told him, "to one of your men."

"Ay, for shooting the guard this morning? 'Twas Will Scathelock. What were you doing at Fountain Dale, lass?"

"Being stupid."

"Ay, well, what's life without a spice of stupidity?" Robin wiped his nose on his sleeve once more; did he *have* to do that? His sleeve looked crusty. He coughed again.

Rowan told him, "You sound worse than yesterday. You should be in a warm bed with a mug of black mullein tea."

"Half my men have colds, and the other half have chills," Robin grumbled. He was losing his voice. "And here I am out in the cold for no better reason than—"

"To play the fool," Rowan put in.

"Nay, surely not! I came to see what we are to do about Queen Elsinor."

Etty wondered, had Rowan sent him word about Mother? Or had Will Scathelock reported the situation in Fountain Dale to him? One way or another, Robin seemed always to know what went on in Sherwood Forest.

And somehow during the interval of his clowning, Etty realized, her mind had made itself up about a few things.

"I found out one thing this morning," she told Robin. "My mother wants me to run—"

"You should," Rook said in his flat way.

Etty shook her head. "No. If I run now, I'll spend my life running from my father. You don't know him."

A petty king. Set upon his own power. Relentless when that power was challenged. "He'll hunt me forever unless I put a stop to him somehow."

Silence. In the valley, frogs chimed like distant bells. Above the budding oaks, a bat buzzed like the insects it fed upon. Far away something snarled. Etty felt many eyes on her as the truth of what she had said hovered like a dark moth in the night.

Rowan murmured, "I see."

"Dear me," Lionel said, "you don't want to spend the rest of your life looking over your shoulder?"

Etty actually smiled, for Lionel knew exactly what she was talking about. He had gone through something of this sort with his father, Lord Roderick Lionclaw, who had put a blood-price of a thousand pounds on his son's head until Lionel had confronted him.

"So you want to stay and fight back," Robin said with both pride and phlegm in his voice.

"Not with weapons. Not if I can help it." Etty wanted no bloodshed. It had been bad enough to see the man-at-arms die today, his simple face looking surprised as a gray goose-feather flower sprouted from his chest.

Rook asked curtly, "Then how?"

"I don't know yet. Robin, you'd better go warm yourself by a fire. I must think of a plan."

Five

Seated on a high crag overlooking Fountain Dale, hidden by holly and keeping a cautious distance, Ettarde watched the encampment below for some hint of what to do. A sign, an omen, a token, anything, Etty didn't know what. Two nights now her mother had been left out in the cold and damp without covering, while Etty had shivered in her mantle and blanket, and frost whitened the stones and ferns in the morning. How much more could Queen Elsinor endure before she caught her death of sickness?

All around, in holly and rowan, wood larks and robins and wrens caroled that it was spring, morning, morning, spring! Ettarde hated them for singing when her mother was suffering. Through the crowns of the oaks below, wreathed with mistletoe but not yet in leaf, Ettarde could see that wretched golden cage and the

entire encampment laid out in small, like the lead fig-
ures in the toy palace she had once played with. No.
Don't think of those days. Think what to do. How to
rescue Mother?

Have Lionel enchant the guards with his singing? No.
They would recognize him and seize him at once. Have
Robin Hood go in disguise? No. He was even more likely
to be recognized than Lionel. Summon the *aelfe,* the spirits of the forest, to help somehow? *I might just as well try
to tell the wild geese what to do.* Etty sighed. She needed
one of Robin Hood's foxy ideas, and Robin's head was too
stuffed with phlegm to give her any. Briefly she reviewed
Plato in her mind, and Herodotus, and Julius Caesar's
history of the Gallic Wars. Nothing in any of them
seemed to apply to the situation of one's mother in a cage.

In the middle of the clearing the golden cage glinted
in the sunlight. Deceitful thing, shining so fair. Etty
could see in it a figure like a tiny white pennon—her
mother, like a flag marking the center of the camp. Off
to one side of Mother, the horses stood tethered to a
line. Off to another side were ranged the wagons and
supplies. In another direction again flowed the well-
spring of water that gave Fountain Dale its name, with
tents pitched nearby for the men-at-arms. And at the
fourth point of the compass, in splendid isolation from
the lesser tents, stood King Solon's pavilion all decked

with rosettes, its canvas freshly painted bright red and white, its pennons fluttering.

And everywhere, guards.

Numbly Ettarde studied their positions, noting how they centered upon her mother's golden cage, three concentric circles of guards. How to rescue her mother? Fly to her through the air? Not unless wings sprouted sometime soon. Burrow to her underground? That would take too long.

It seemed hopeless.

Yet Etty stayed where she was, frowning down on the encampment as if it were a puzzle she could solve somehow. The sun rose higher, drying the melted frost from crags and bracken and prickly holly leaves. The wood larks flew away, the robins and wrens quieted. Hawks circled in the high sky. Down below, a few travelers walked the Nottingham Way. A peasant driving a yoke of oxen. A charcoal burner with his load of wood piled on his donkey. A dark-cloaked figure . . .

Etty stiffened, wondering if it might be Robin Hood in his idiotic disguise again. But no, this was a smaller man, and she could see his matted beard hanging. It truly was one of those accursed Wanderers this time. One of those roaming foreigners with their black hair and black eyes and their sad, narrow faces. At the sight of him, Etty's nose wrinkled as if she smelled something bad. She felt entitled to sneer, for everyone hated the thieving, begging Wanderers with their hoards of gold. Everyone said they lent gold to rich lords, and demanded human flesh in return. Folk said that they stole babies from cradles and raised them to be witches. Folk said they possessed the evil eye, and that if one of them walked between two men, one of those men would die.

Etty did not believe in the evil eye. But the beggary, the thievery, the hidden riches, these were common knowledge. She could see how the soldiers down below had frozen like songbirds when the hawk flies over, silent and wary as the accursed one passed. Etty's lip curled like her nose as she watched the dark-robed figure slip by.

Once it was out of sight, her body relaxed. Time inched on. Etty sighed. Had the sun ever before moved so slowly in the sky?

Along came a peddler in a cart, trundling by almost as slowly as the sun. Later came a swineherd driving his pigs, and later yet, a knight with his squire trailing him. All turned their heads to stare at the encampment, the lady in her cage. Etty felt her face burn with mortification for her mother.

Otherwise she took small interest in the travelers, even the knight shining in his mail, even a page boy on an aristocratic white pony. Etty did give a moment's regard to the pony, slim and sleek and pretty, for even at a distance she could see the bright yellow plumes nodding between its ears, matching the plumes in the page boy's hat above his long, curling yellow hair. Quite the dandy he was, what with the hat and the hair and a tight crimson tunic and perfectly fitted yellow hose above tall leather boots. Etty blinked as she saw him enter the encampment, sweeping off his hat as he approached her father's canvas castle of a pavilion. But then she forgot about him. Some lord's messenger, that was all.

The sun crawled like a yellow snail toward noon. Somewhere, monotonously, a cuckoo began to call. Annoying bird. It laid its eggs in other birds' nests. Backdoor bird, folk called it, because of the way it came and went when no one was watching. If a man's wife were unfaithful, folk mocked him: Cuckoo! Cuckoo! Calling him a cuckold because someone had been sneaking in his back door.

Bracken rustled slightly, and Etty heard a panting sound. She turned, then smiled. Tykell, her escort today, stood waving his plumy tail and breathing his meaty breath in her face. He licked her ear, then turned around three times and lay down on the sun-warmed rock beside her.

"Ready for a nap, Ty?" Etty murmured, stroking his thick fur. But her smile did not last. Down below she

44

saw that her father had emerged from his pavilion. Father, like a lead soldier—no, an itsy-bitsy leaden king—was stalking around the encampment and, judging by the way he flailed his arms, roaring orders.

The cuckoo kept calling. "Hush," Etty muttered.

"Cuckoo!" It perched almost over her head now, in the holly, so close she could see its sleek gray feathers, its beady amber eye, its yellow bill gaping as it called. "Cuckoo!"

"My father's not a cuckold." Mother was a virtuous woman. All the more reason that Father should not be treating her this way. "Go away, backdoor bird—"

Etty gasped, and her eyes widened. The cuckoo did not go away, but she forgot all about it, sitting bolt upright, staring at the scene below. Mother seemed to be lying down on the hard, bare floor of the cage, maybe warming herself in the sunshine, maybe even napping. Nothing else had changed. But Etty whispered, "Yes! That's it!"

Stiff from her vigil, she struggled to her feet. "Ty," she told the wolf-dog, "I am an idiot. Come on, let's go find the others."

"I am an idiot!" she cried to the others when Ty had led her to them. They took no notice, preoccupied by the task at hand. In a secluded glade of Sherwood

45

Forest, they were butchering a deer. The air smelled of new green leaves and violets in bud and innards and blood. Ettarde did not mind the guts and blood, but she noticed that Lionel did; he stood with his back to the deer—even though he had shot it, apparently. The skin lay at his feet. "Your kill?" Ettarde demanded.

Lionel nodded. "Better one full-grown stag than a dozen yearlings," he grumbled.

There it hung by its hocks from the limb of an oak, its elegant head dragging on the ground, looking silvery naked with its skin off. Robin and a couple of his men were doing the butchering. They would receive a share of the meat, Etty knew, for this was not a fallow deer or a roebuck; it was a massive red-deer stag, with so much meat it would spoil before Rowan's small band could eat it all.

"Well done. Even your great belly could not eat so much venison," Etty teased, trying to cheer Lionel. He hated to kill. But someone had to, if the band was to eat. Rook brought in fish he caught with his bare hands, but it was not enough. Etty could shoot a bow, but she was no hunter. And Rowan, a fine hunter, could not yet follow the deer. She was still limping. Also, Rowan had all the gathering of herbs to see to. So it was left to poor overgrown-baby Lionel to kill game for meat. Etty smiled to herself, knowing that she and the others would hear Lionel lament for days now.

Rowan saw the smile and returned it, perhaps thinking the same thing. Sitting with a mass of mistletoe in her lap, she plucked its cure-all leaves, which had to be gathered before the berries appeared. Next Rowan would be looking for nettles to heal sores, then mallow and mullein for poultices and colds, agrimony and camomile for fever and bellyache. And holly and hyssop and coltsfoot and comfrey.

"I am an idiot," Etty told her.

"How so?" Rowan inquired gravely. "I have no cure for idiocy."

Forgetting to be either a princess or an outlaw, Etty bounced in place like a puppy. "I *was* an idiot, but I have it now!"

They all turned to her—all except Tykell, who began devouring scraps. Rowan put aside her mistletoe. Rook, who had started scraping Lionel's deerskin for him, stilled his knife. Robin stood with his jerkin sleeves rolled up and his bare arms bloody, organ meats in his hands. "Have what, lass?" His voice sounded hoarse from his cold.

Lionel demanded, "You know how to rescue your mother?"

"Yes. No. I mean, not exactly. Sort of through the back door."

They stared at her blankly.

"Back door," Etty repeated as if they were quite dense not to understand. "All I was thinking is Mother, Mother, rescue Mother. But I can't. Father has her at the center of Fountain Dale, with all the guards in the world stationed around her. But *his* pavilion is off at the edge of the clearing. There are a few guards, but they won't be expecting us. If someone can make a little diversion at the far end of the dale . . ." Etty looked at Robin Hood, then at Rowan. "An odd noise or something, just enough to distract the guards but not enough to make them raise the alarm, then Lionel and I can get to him before—"

"Now, wait!" Lionel peered at her. "My dear lady, why me?"

"I'm *not* your dear lady. Why you? Because you're big enough to carry him off."

"But—but—but—"

"Lionel, no more *but*s! You know you're going to do it."

Rowan said in her soft way, "Instead of rescuing your mother, we capture your father?"

"Yes!"

"And his ransom will be her release."

"Exactly."

"Well thought!" Robin was beginning to grin, even as he coughed into his rolled jerkin sleeve. "'Tis a worthy plan, forsooth. But does he keep no guards in his tent, lass?"

"My father? No. He hates people."

"But he'll slice us to bits!" Lionel burst out.

"That's *your* father, Lionel. My father is a scholar, not the kind who sleeps with his sword. He thinks too much to make a proper king. He's afraid of the dark."

"No! Truly?" Robin exclaimed.

"Truly. He's noble on the outside but a coward within." *The opposite of Lionel,* Etty thought. "He won't fight us. We must see that he does not cry out, that's all."

Rowan murmured, "It sounds almost too easy."

"And afterward?" Robin asked. "What are we to do with our good king Solon the Red, lass?"

"I'd like to hang him up like yonder deer!" Etty sighed, blowing away her sudden anger, then spoke with the calm her mother had trained into her. "But I suppose I must somehow make him let my mother go. And let me be."

Six

In the darkest mid of night an owl gave its ghostly call. A fox barked. A mouse squeaked. Etty, who was the mouse, knew that the fox (Robin Hood) and the owl (Rowan) had taken their positions. In a moment it would be time to move.

Crouching in the shadow of a giant oak tree with Rook on one side and Lionel on the other, Etty focused just to one side of the guard she was trying to watch. Trying to see in a moonless, cloudy night was like trying to see a dim star. The guards near Mother's cage kept fires going to warm themselves and to see intruders by, but at this end of the clearing there was only a whisper of firelight, and in the woods not even that. By not looking directly at the guard, Etty could just barely see him standing about ten paces away, yawning, at the edge of the clearing, between her and the back of her father's pavilion.

Father, lying asleep so near her . . . Without warning, Etty's thoughts jolted back to when she was a child, her father's little princess and his little scholar. Lacking any surviving sons, he had taught all his learning to her, even though girls were hardly ever educated. He would summon her to his throne and show her off before visiting lords. Had he . . . was it possible he had loved her then? Or had she been just another of his prized possessions, like his golden drinking goblet or his well-trained horse?

It doesn't matter, Etty told herself, jerking her thoughts back to the present. Most assuredly he did not love her now.

And she would never be anyone's possession again.

Where was that guard? There. Still in the same place.

From the far side of the clearing voices sounded. Guards calling to each other.

"What was that?"

"A wolf!"

"No, a dog, fool. What would a wolf be doing—"

"It's a wolf, I say! Shoot it!"

Ettarde smiled to herself, listening, knowing what would happen next. She and Rowan and the others had grown accustomed to what had once seemed almost un-believable.

Sure enough, the man shouted, "The brute caught my arrow!"

"Fool, what are you talking about?"

"He caught it in his mouth! Snatched it right out of the air."

"This I have to see. Shoot another."

The guard turned his head to see what was going on, then left his post to get a better look. It sounded as though most of the guards, if not all of them, were gathering at the far end of the clearing to watch Tykell leaping to clamp his jaws onto arrow after arrow, snagging them in midflight like a swift darting after mayflies.

Signaling Rook and Lionel by touching their hands, Etty ran forward as silently as she could. She could hear Rook loping almost soundlessly on his bare feet and Lionel thudding along behind her—the big lout, surely the guards would hear him! But no one raised the alarm as she sprinted through the hazel bushes and across a few paces of open clearing to crouch, breathing hard, in the shadow behind her father's pavilion. She could hear the wild boy and the oversized minstrel panting beside her.

Then there was a ripping sound. As planned, Lionel was cutting a way into the pavilion with his dagger.

Soft yellow light spilled through the rent: candle glow. Within the tent, an expensive beeswax candle stood burning uselessly in the middle of the night. Mirthless, Etty smiled. Yes, her father still required his candle for comfort in order to sleep. Likely he still required his sleeping draughts, too.

As Lionel cautiously spread the opening he had made in the canvas, Etty could see her father lying there with his pointed beard in the air and his hands symmetrically tucked under his chin, over the coverlet.

Etty touched Lionel's arm, then stepped softly inside the tent.

The other two catfooted after her. Soft deerskin boots made little noise. Silently Etty begged the spirits of the night, *Please, let him sleep like a fish under ice until we get our hands on him.* He must not awaken and summon the guards.

King Solon's pavilion was a rich sort of tent, well hung with draperies to please the eye and to mute noises from outside. Etty could hear the guards only faintly now:

" 'Tis a full wondrous wolf, forsooth."

"Look! Yon friendly wolf wishes to greet the lady."

"Go ahead, my lady. Reach through the bars and pat him."

And then her mother's courteous voice:

"Welcome, Sir Wolf. Or should it be Lord Wolf? Are you the wolf ruler of this wilderness?"

Etty's heart beat harder as she heard her mother's voice, harder and faster as she drifted forward silently, oh so silently, to position herself at her sleeping father's head. Just as silently, Lionel stood at his side, and Rook at his feet. Etty met their eyes and nodded. *Now!*

All three at once seized King Solon. He awoke with what would have been a shriek but was only a squeak, for Etty had clamped both her hands over his mouth. He tried to thrash, but Rook leaned on his feet and Lionel held both of his hands easily in one of his own, binding them with a thong of cured deerskin.

Etty glanced down at her father's face. He saw her, and his mouth squirmed and mumbled under her hands, and his pale eyes met hers with such fearsome upside-down fury that she flinched as if she had encountered a viper. Hastily she looked away from him. "Gag him," she whispered to Lionel, although she knew he was not finished with his own task yet.

From somewhere in back of the draperies that lined the pavilion, behind Lionel, a high-pitched, sleepy voice asked, "What passes here?"

Etty startled so hard she almost lost her hold on her father's mouth. And Lionel jumped even harder, losing his hold on His Majesty's half-bound hands entirely.

Rook reached over and seized the end of the thong. Lionel spun around. Etty froze. All three of them gawked at the face gawking back at them from between the draperies.

A delicate, narrow face with great dark eyes under masses of curling hair paler than the candlelight. Never had Etty seen a human being with such black eyes and such blond hair. "It's the page boy," she gasped. Still in his crimson tunic, it was the dandified messenger she had seen riding in on the slender white pony. And had not thought of since.

His mouth started to open, to scream.

In a single giant stride Lionel was upon him, clapping one big hand over his mouth as he seized him around the arms and body. "*Certainly*, your father hates people," Lionel hissed at Etty as he hauled the page boy out of the draperies to the center of the tent. "*Absolutely*, he always sleeps alone—"

"Shhh!" Etty had seen the page boy's dark eyes widen. "Idiot, now he knows who I am."

"As if they don't all know—"

Rook interrupted. "Hush. Bind him. We must take him, too, or he'll betray us."

Why, Etty wondered, should binding and gagging two prisoners take three times as long? But it seemed to.

In fact it seemed to take forever. Rook had to sit on King Solon's legs and finish tying his hands while he squirmed and grunted muffled threats from under Etty's grip, while Lionel kept his hold on the page boy. Then Rook had to pull back the blankets and tie the king's feet. Any other time Etty would have giggled at the sight of her oh-so-dignified father in his small-clothes, but now she could think only of the passing of time. "Hurry!" she whispered as Rook went to get the gag from Lionel.

"Shhh."

Finally it was done. Etty's father lay mute and furious, gagged and bound hand and foot, as Etty scrambled to help Rook and Lionel with the page boy. Hastily they bound his hands with the cross-garters from Lionel's leggings. Even more hastily they gagged him with the same. With small ceremony Lionel slung King Solon of Auberon over his shoulder and bolted, ducking out the back door he had cut in the pavilion. Hustling the page boy between them, each with a hand under one of his arms, Etty and Rook followed.

Dark, too dark. After candlelight, nothing but blackness out there. No time to let the eyes adjust. Etty could see nothing. The twenty paces to the cover of the forest seemed to take a year. Straining her ears, Etty could hear nothing but the roaring of her own pulse. Where were the guards? Still playing with Tykell? Or—

"Halt!" roared a man's voice close at hand. "Who goes there?"

That challenge pierced Etty like an arrow. Heart pounding, she ducked behind the first big oak at the edge of the forest, hauling Rook and the page boy with her. Too much time had passed, the diversion had ceased to divert, and now the guard would sound the alarm, Robin and his men would have to come to the rescue, there would be blood—

The guard bellowed, "Answer, or I shoot!"

Etty sensed more than saw that her captive gave a twisting motion of his head. She jumped like a squirrel when his voice sounded, piping loud and peevish, from right beside her.

"*Mon foi*, porridge-face," he cried, "it is I, Beauregard du Fleur Noir. What mean you, *bête gross odieux*, to shout at me? You'll wake the king."

Feeling a trifle dizzy, Etty leaned against the oak.

"Young master? What are you doing out here?" The guard lowered his voice, but Etty could hear him walking nearer. And she could hear other voices and footsteps approaching, more guards joining the first. Biting her lip, she reached for the dagger in her belt.

The page boy retorted, "Radish-head, what you think? I sniff the night breezes, *non*?"

"The latrines are beyond the tents—"

"Pah!" The page boy's voice became imperious. "You think I take my breeches down for the common filth holes? Go milk yourself. I tell the king—"

"As you will, Master Beauregard. I beg your pardon." The guard retreated, taking the others with him.

Etty breathed out.

She listened to the footsteps and voices fading away. For about ten heartbeats there was blessed, utter silence. Then, from somewhere close at hand in the darkness, Lionel whispered, "Who tied that gag on him?"

Keeping his voice very soft now, the page boy himself answered. "The princess Ettarde. I think she desire not to hurt me, *oui*?"

"*Oui*," Etty agreed. "I mean, yes."

She felt him press something into her hands in the darkness—the strips of cloth that had bound him. He had slipped right out of them. "I come with you," he told her. "We go now, *oui*?"

"*Oui*. Um, yes."

Seven

A pretty sight, forsooth! But what is it?" Eyes twinkling like blue stars in the firelight, Robin gazed at the page boy.

Etty smiled back at Robin Hood, gave him a quick kiss on the cheek, then sat down with a sigh of relief on the ground under the huge, hollow oak tree where Robin and his men customarily made camp. Rook remained standing, and so did the page boy. Let them stand. The males could keep their useless pride. Etty was tired and she would admit to it, so tired she could have lain down right on the damp ground. It had been a long, weary nighttime trudge to Robin's favorite hideout, but necessary to get well away from Fountain Dale.

Ignoring Robin's question for the moment, Etty asked, "Have you seen Lionel?"

"Poor wee Lionel? Aye, he's halfway between here and there with his leggings flapping."

"He thinks he can carry Father all this way—"

"He can't. But Little John is helping him." Robin coughed and wiped his nose on the usual place, his jerkin sleeve. Feeling Etty's disapproving glance, he gave a wry smile. "Sorry. No kerchiefs in the wildwood, barring the one that belongs to a certain pretty lady. Throw some more wood on the fire, lads," he told the outlaws who had gathered around to survey the visitors, "and bring forth that excellent venison. So, Etty, explain." Robin scanned the page boy with his most quizzical grin. "This is a pretty bird of unexpected feather."

"No salt on our tails, thanks to him," Etty replied.

"Beauregard du Fleur Noir, *a votre service,*" said the page boy in his flutelike voice, reaching for his yellow-plumed cap, which was not there. He made a deep bow anyway, sweeping the imaginary hat.

There was a muttering among Robin's men. "Frank-ish," Etty heard someone whisper.

"Sissy Frankish boy," mumbled somebody else.

Frankish, yes. Sissy? Etty recalled that they had all once thought Lionel a sissy.

"Should have been a girl," grumbled another outlaw.

They scorn him because he's beautiful, Etty thought, noticing how the firelight played on Beauregard's silvery skin, outlining his profile in gold. A classical Grecian profile, worthy of a cameo, with its elegant brow flowing straight into an aristocratic nose. Beautiful, those sloe-black glowing eyes under curls even fairer than Robin Hood's. This Beauregard was worthy of a ballad.

"*Enchanté* to you encounter, Robin of the Hood," he said as he completed his bow. "*Quel plaisir*. I—"

"The pleasure is mine." Robin anticipated fun, Etty could tell by the glint in his blue eyes. "Just so long as you don't call me porridge-face or *bête gross odieux*."

Etty sat bolt upright with a gasp. "You heard!"

Robin just grinned.

"We wondered what was taking you so long." With Tykell at her heels, Rowan appeared beside Robin. "We came to see."

Beauregard acknowledged Rowan at once. "*Enchanté*, mademoiselle." He bowed so deeply that Tykell sniffed his nose. Beauregard straightened. Tykell wagged his bushy tail as Beauregard asked Rowan, "*Vous êtes* the handmaiden of the princess Ettarde?"

"No!" said Ettarde.

"Yes," said Rowan. Despite this outrageous fib, she faced Beauregard with her usual grave, level gaze. "They found you in the pavilion?"

61

"He found us," Etty put in. "Caught us in the act."

Beauregard said, "The big Lionel, he grab me, *oui*, but not hurt."

Robin Hood asked, "But why were you there, lad?"

"Sleeping! The fools did not wish it, but *mon foi*, I would not let them put me with the common soldiers. Brrr!" Beauregard shuddered expressively, and Etty heard a muttering go around the outlaws again. Rook growled as Tykell had not, and turned away.

"Well," Robin said with sobriety worthy of an owl, "you'll be pleased to know there are no common fellows here. This is Prince William of Scathelock—" Robin gave a ladylike wave of the hand toward one of the outlaws standing at his back, then the next. "—and Lord Much of Millerson, and His Highness Emperor Rafe—"

Beauregard interrupted. "I understand, mine prince of outlaws." He drew himself up to his full height, such as it was, so that his head almost reached the level of Robin's chin. "You joke me, but *sacre bleu*, it is yet true, the woodland freedom make royalty of you all."

Watching the page boy's beautiful face, Etty lifted her head in interest. Was that a glimmer of mischief in Beauregard's black eyes? Robin thought he was playing with the boy, but who was playing with whom?

Will Scathelock was not amused by anyone's foolery. "I'm no prince," he growled at Beauregard. "We're all yeomen here. If you scorn common—"

Robin turned his head, saying quietly, "Let it go, Will. Get him something to eat. Remember what he did earlier tonight."

For the matter of that . . . "Beauregard," Etty demanded, "why did you help us?"

In one easy move he swiveled to kneel before her, yellow tights and tall boots and all. He had worn his boots to sleep in?

"*Quel dommage*. A shame," he said quite softly. "It is a great shame to King Solon, my princess, that he has put the sweet lady in the cage."

But how many men, or boys either, would take such a risk just because they thought something was a shame? This Beauregard had aided outlaws, and would very likely be outlawed in his turn. Did he not realize what he was doing? Etty stared into the shadowy midnight pools that were the page boy's eyes, frowning.

"*Mon foi*," he protested against her silence, "I adore to be outlaw like you, Princess Ettarde."

He knew, then. Who she was. But he was, or had been, the high king's messenger. Was he also the high king's spy?

His courtesy felt false, overdone, excessive even by the standards to which Etty had been raised. It felt like mockery.

"Don't call me princess," she told him. "Do I look like a princess to you?" Certainly she had all her teeth and no pockmarks on her skin, but if that made her a princess, then he was a prince, for he could say the same. But how could he call her princess when she had fleabites all over her arms, when her head itched with lice, when she was sitting there in deerskin boots and a green kirtle with a deerskin belt, with her hair pulled back in a thong?

Once again Beauregard reached for his hat as if to sweep it in a gallant gesture. "But you are the very princess of the wildwood," he said.

This boy beauty had an answer for everything. Etty studied him, blinking, then glanced up toward Robin and Rowan, seeing the same doubt in both their faces that she felt in her own. There was something unrevealed about this Beauregard.

Far off in the forest a wagtail whistled. Robin turned his head, and Etty stood up, looking and listening. There came the sound of brush rustling, twigs breaking, distant at first but drawing nearer. With a commotion worthy of a rampaging lion, a tall, top-heavy form appeared, looking like a hunchback because of the load he carried—Etty could see Lionel, she realized, better than firelight allowed. A whisper of light was dawning in the sky. It was daybreak.

Far more quietly, a tall, green-clad outlaw strode into the clearing that encircled Robin's spreading oak. Little John, all towering seven feet of him. He gave Robin a nod to signify that all was well.

Stumbling up to Etty, Lionel eased his burden to the ground. There lay King Solon, glaring pale-eyed over the gag in his mouth, with his beard in a spiky mess and goose bumps on his bare, hairy legs. Etty stared. It was like encountering a strange animal she had never even heard of before. For just a moment she felt sorry for the poor creature, so scared and cold—but then her pity flared into anger. It was her father, and had he felt sorry for her when he had starved her? Had he felt sorry for her when he had sent her off to be married to an ugly old toad of a lord?

Did he love her? At all?

A loud groan sounded. Etty stiffened and looked to see who was hurt. Oh. No matter, it was just Lionel. "My back is broken," he lamented, flopping full length on the ground. "That so-called king looks like a grasshopper, but he weighs like an ox."

No one paid any attention, for Lionel lived to complain. They all stood in a circle around the captive, looking down at him. His arms were hairy, too, with goose bumps. Etty no longer noticed his glare, for she had focused instead on his smallclothes. They looked far from white, and needed mending. Imagine, a king with holey smalls.

"Well," said Robin Hood after a while, "here's your prisoner, Etty, lass. Now what?"

Eight

With all eyes upon her, Etty blinked at Robin Hood, feeling as if her brain had turned into mashed turnips. In the great oak spreading overhead, thrushes and whitethroats and wrens sang of sunrise and spring, nests and mating and bugs and fledglings. And the chaffinches wondered: What? What? What ho, what? they sang. *What, indeed?* Etty thought. Robin expected *her* to take charge?

True, she had very much taken charge till now . . . but she had not thought much beyond the capture. Her father lay trussed like a cooked goose at her feet, glaring up at her, and—

And staring back at him, Etty felt her muddled thoughts turn sharp and cold like splintered ice. Turning to Robin, she inquired sweetly, "Have we a cage? I would like to put him in a cage in his smalls and give him bread and water to eat. Let folk stare at him. Leave him there to spend his nights in the cold."

Out of the tail of her eye she saw her father's glare widen into a startled stare. She ignored him.

Others were staring at her also. Beauregard, Rook, Lionel, Rowan, Robin. Etty realized they had never seen her truly angry—no, more: enraged. Yet she would not shout. She was too much her mother's daughter to rage aloud.

"No cage?" she went on just as cooly to Robin. "Very well, we shall chain him to a tree instead. Shackles on his hands and shackles on his bare ankles. But let us shave his beard first—"

"Etty, stop it," said a gentle voice, Rowan's.

"Why? I am quite serious. We must shave his beard to let folk see what a sorry chin he has under it. Then—"

Rowan moved to stand before her, laying quiet hands on either side of her head.

"I don't want healing! Let me be." Etty lifted her hands to push Rowan away. But in the next breath she felt—better, blast it all. Tension like a bowstring across her shoulders started to relax. She had not even noticed something buzzing like a thousand locusts in her mind until the noise eased into silence. Under Rowan's touch, intimations of peace bloomed in her heart.

For a moment, Etty really felt the new-day sunshine warming her shoulders.

Rowan lifted her hands and faced her levelly, gesturing at her father. "You wish to be like him?" she asked.

"No!" Etty swallowed and spoke more calmly. "No. I don't. Toads take you, Rowan."

The outlaw girl smiled as warm as the sunrise. "I'll get our guest a blanket," she said. "He's cold." She limped toward Robin's oak.

"Have your men unbind King Solon," Etty told Robin in her normal tone, although wearily, "and let him warm himself by the fire, and give him something to eat."

"My curse on all of you!" King Solon raged as the outlaws removed the gag from his mouth. "Get your hands off me, dirty churls!" as they seated him on a heap of soft doeskins at the guest's place of honor upon the mossy roots of the great oak, with the campfire near his feet. "A pox take you!" as they unbound his wrists and served him venison with mushroom gravy for breakfast.

Standing nearby, Etty turned her back to all this, feeling tired. Very tired. No wonder. She hadn't slept.

"Are you all right, lass?" Robin asked, walking up to her.

She nodded, wondering hazily what he meant. Why should she not be all right?

"Well, then, we need to think what to do next. May my yeomen rest, or must I keep them at the ready? How long will it take your father's retainers to come looking for him?"

"I don't know," Etty admitted.

An unexpected voice spoke. "It will take them the better part of the day, if not longer." Beauregard, seated on the ground with his booted feet thrust out, gestured with a hunk of bread in his slender white hand. "The men of our good King Solon, they are grumbling," he said. "They have not been paid, and the food is poor. The captain is old, the sergeant challenges him at every turn, and the men do no more than they have to."

Robin wheeled to peer at him. "How do you know all this, lad?"

"I heard and saw. Yesterday."

Etty found herself wide-awake within a moment. "What has become of your Frankish accent?" she demanded.

A grin as bright and sudden as lightning flashed on his fine-boned face. His black eyes glinted with fun. "*Mes yeux,* mademoiselle," he said. "*Merci beaucoup* for to remind me."

"Please forget that she reminded you." Robin eyed

the page boy thoughtfully. "Master Beauregard—if that is indeed your name—why did the high king send you here?"

"Ah, it is just a small matter of taxes." He waved his breakfast languidly. "King Solon has not paid them."

"For that, you followed Solon *here*? To Sherwood Forest?"

"*Oui*, most assuredly." Beauregard grinned again. "The better part of my task is to spy. King Solon is in much difficulty."

Etty peered at Beauregard, feeling certain now that the stranger boy liked to rattle the bushes. He meant his foppish clothes and his so-called Frankish accent to annoy any yeomen who would judge him shallowly. Or perhaps he was actually mocking the dandies of the high king's Frankish court. He was a gadfly, with a kind of nerve new to Ettarde. Intent on him, she moved a few steps closer, so that she looked down at the top of his golden head.

"You have the high king's ear," Robin was saying to Beauregard, "yet you would throw in your lot with outlaws? But you could have risen—"

"Beauregard," Etty blurted, interrupting in her surprise, "your hair is as fair as flax, but the roots are raven black."

The boy dropped his bread as his hands jerked up,

trying to cover his head in the absence of his hat. His dark eyes widened, all their glitter gone, leaving only stark fear.

And Robin sucked in his breath with a hiss, stepping back as if he had seen an adder. "Guards!" he called sharply. Will Scathelock was already standing by. "Much, Rafe, John!"

"*Mon foi*," faltered Beauregard, regaining some of his poise, "a simple potion turns the hair yellow to charm the ladies, what is the harm of that?"

Etty gawked. He had changed the color of his hair? She had never heard of such a thing. But still, as he had said, what harm—

"He's a black-haired blackguard," said Will Scathelock, as harsh as flint. "He's one of the foul folk. A Wanderer."

Etty stiffened as knowledge broke upon her, truth as sharp as glass shattering. That narrow face like a carving from—from somewhere ancient, Greece, Egypt— that head like a sleek cat's poised atop a fine neck, those winglike cheekbones, that elegant unbroken line of brow and nose . . .

"You are one of the accursed race," Etty whispered, edging back, feeling the knowledge ripple up her back, clenching every muscle.

"Accursed! For what cause?" Beauregard rose, his

black eyes flashing, all his foppery gone. "My race holds no land, makes no wars, sheds no blood. No man of my race holds any other man slave or serf or servant. You call us thieves? It is true we steal sometimes, to survive, but are you not also thieves, O outlaws?" He shot a level look that took in Will Scathelock, Robin, all of them.

"Silence." Etty had never seen Robin so stern. "You have come here in disguise, to deceive me—"

"Have you not also gone about in disguise?"

Outlaws shouted with rage. Will drew his short sword. "How dare you! As if he were like you?"

Others cried out. "Bah! You sneaking villain!"

"You of the wicked race—"

"Bloody-handed—"

"Cradle robber—"

But Beauregard's flutelike voice pierced through them all. "You think we steal babies? Bah, what for? Who needs more?" He tossed his head, arrow-straight and defiant. "We steal gold, given a chance—but the greatest thieves of all, are they not the kings and so-called lords of *your* race? Stealing livelihood and soul from common folk, wresting maidens from their fathers?"

"Enough," Robin commanded. He turned to Will and the others. "Will, sheathe your sword. Take him within." Inside the oak, he meant. Its hollow could house a dozen outlaws in a huddle. Robin ordered, "Do not mistreat him, but guard him well, and tell him nothing."

Etty watched Beauregard's proud, straight back, shoulders square under the crimson tunic, as they took him away. "I *liked* him," she whispered, shuddering.

Robin let out a long breath. "Use your head, lass," he told her gently enough, "not just your heart."

Nine

Etty knew she had to do it.

With a wavering feeling in her gut, but keeping her face calm, she walked up to the fire and seated herself facing her father. His breakfast, she noticed, lay beside him upon its trencher, untouched. Glaring wildly behind him, as if something might be sneaking up on him, he did not see her sit down almost near enough to touch.

Firming her voice, Etty spoke. "Father."

With a jerk he faced her, his sharp red eyebrows bunched like wings. He opened his mouth.

"Father," Etty said before he could start scolding, "you will send orders for Mother to be clothed, fed and released. At once."

She saw his face go meat red, dark beneath the carrot color of his beard. But he kept control of his rage, letting it give force to his words as he told her too softly, "Foolish girl, your impudence will be punished. Your mother will die."

Inside herself, Etty felt little Princess Ettarde quivering like frog eggs. Papa really did possess the power, legally, to have Mama killed. Yet outwardly, Etty did not tremble, for she was an outlaw now. She said, "Remember what Seneca said, Father: All cruelty springs from weakness."

It was her father who had taught her to read and memorize her Latin and Greek. He had provided a whipping girl to be beaten with a dog lash when Ettarde did not learn her lessons, and it had been harder for Ettarde to watch the peasant girl cry than it would have been to take her own punishment. Papa was like that—perverse, somehow cruel even in kindness. And proud, all too ready to show off his wealth or his horses or his learned daughter before his honored guests. A daughter who could read and write, forsooth! But above all, Father was proud of his own learning.

The only way to defeat Father, Etty sensed, to really defeat him in his heart, would be to conquer him with the weapons he had taught her. With words. The Romans, the Greeks.

But he always wins the debates! Always!

Not this time, Etty told herself. Not with the help of

the coolness her mother had taught her and the defiance she had learned from the outlaws.

Seated across the fire from King Solon the Red, and taking care to appear at ease, Etty helped herself to some fresh wheat bread.

Her father aimed his forefinger at her like a spear. "You munch bread in my presence like a dairymaid? No daughter of mine is a coarse, common—"

"*Argumentum ad hominem,*" Etty told him, reaching for some of Robin's dark, wild honey to go with the bread.

"You overspeak yourself, ungrateful wench, just because I gave you an education. It is as Socrates said: Once woman is made equal to man, she fancies herself his superior."

"In more honest translation, Father, Socrates declared that educated woman *is* superior to man." Etty licked honey from her fingers.

"Have you forgotten how Semonides compares woman to a hairy sow, a braying donkey, a vixen?"

"And whom would you rather contemplate, Father, Semonides or Socrates? Or Plato? Have you forgotten how Plato and Xenophon argue that the soul is without gender, and woman is therefore the moral equal of man?"

"But not the legal equal!"

"Yes, in Plato's *Republic,* the legal equal also, to be educated alongside the men, take physical training like men, and share in the responsibilities of state."

"Bah. You believe in such a fairy-tale world?" King Solon the Red drew himself up and fixed his daughter with his most stern and regal stare. "Speak truth, girl: Do you consider yourself my equal?"

Etty had learned to her bones the code of Sherwood Forest: An outlaw is the equal of anyone. Therefore, although her knees trembled under her skirt, it was not too difficult for her to placidly reply, "Absolutely, Father. And in some ways, your superior."

His face flushed crimson above his orange hedgehog beard. He stiffened like a barking dog. "Strumpet!" he howled. "Shameless vandal of good taste and tradition!"

There. He had lost his temper. She had breached his fortifications, at least.

Etty became aware that outlaws had gathered around the fire, listening, that Robin stood grinning behind King Solon, that Rowan had settled beside her with a quiet smile, and that she, Etty, was almost enjoying herself, enraging her father.

But she had not brought him here to enjoy herself.

Or even to defeat him in debate, really. She had broken down his defenses somewhat, but . . . how to find the man inside?

Had he ever loved Mother? At all?

Did he ever love me?

Etty sighed, set her food aside and wiped her hands on her kerchief. She faced her father levelly, inwardly begging him to hear her. She looked into his hawkish eyes—had she ever dared to really look into his eyes before? They surprised her. Hard, yes, but also old and bleak.

Etty asked quietly, "If I am such a disgrace to you, Father, why do you want me back? Why not leave me here?"

He replied too quickly, without thought. "Because, in the proper order of things, the father should exercise authority over his family, and the king—"

A flare of rage took Etty by surprise. "Is that what you call it?" She could not keep her face from hardening as her voice turned ice sharp. "You call it authority, to punish and humiliate your wife, who has done nothing but serve you, whom you should cherish the most—"

"You speak like a child." Back in control, King Solon showed his teeth in a cold smile. "Have you forgotten your Thucydides? The powerful take what they can, and the weak give what they must. Woman is weak—"

"Only in the narrowest sense of the word. In other ways, man is weaker." Confound everything, she had lost her advantage, and he was back on his high horse. Within an eye blink, Etty changed tactics. "Tell me, Father, why are there holes in your smallclothes?"

She could not have appalled him more if she had spit. He jerked upright and gasped for breath. "How dare you! I—"

"You lack a few coppers to spend for the making of new ones. Why so?"

With his red eyebrows bunched fit to fly, he glared at her without speaking. She stared back at him. From the far side of the oak, she heard the laughter and talk of outlaws. A mistle thrush ranted from a high branch, and in the sky overhead, a hawk screamed. But around the campfire, all was silence.

Etty said at last, "Lord Basil is pressing you hard, is that it?"

"Aye!" The answer exploded out of him. "If you had married him as I bade you, to ally our families, all would have been well. But since you willfully disobeyed me—"

"Have you not reared me to possess my own mind? Now should I take poison if you command me to?"

King Solon ignored this, ranting on, releasing truth at last. "Since you wed him not, all has fallen to ruin. His army is three times the size of mine. Already last autumn he took from me the better part of my lands. And now that spring is here, he will soon besiege Auberon itself."

"Oh," Etty whispered, for she was beginning to surmise what he wanted of her.

"Because you have been an undutiful daughter," he said with his teeth glinting amid his bristling beard, "folk will starve and soldiers will die."

Etty felt weak. Visions flashed in her mind of terrified peasants running from their homes, of crops and villages in flames, of soldiers bloodily dying and castle walls falling, of rude strangers brawling into Auberon, tearing the tapestries, into her tower chamber, tossing her books into the fire, into her home—

No. Sherwood Forest was her home now.

"But perhaps it is not too late," her father was saying with an edge like a rat's bite in his voice. "Lord Basil might yet be mollified if you submit yourself to him in wedlock."

Etty felt Rowan's gentle touch on her hand. That contact seemed like the only real thing in the world, the only thing that kept her from whirling away in a wind of nightmare. Her father's high-browed face swam before her eyes, his pallid skin stretched like parchment over the skull of his forehead.

"You quote the philosophers," he was saying. "What would Socrates or any of the rest of them say now? Just by doing your duty to me as a daughter, you could save many lives."

"Etty," Rowan whispered, "no. It's all wrong."

Was it wrong? It felt wrong, yet . . . Etty shook her head, trying to clear it, but the thought would not go away. All her father wanted of her was sacrifice. And sacrifice was noble, was it not?

Ten

Sacrifice. Etty knew her duty: to give herself, the way most women did, the way Mother had always given and given of herself. . . .

Mother.

In that cage of Father's making.

Have Father command Mother's release? When sky turned brown and earth turned blue, maybe it would happen. But till then, somebody had better do something.

Etty's feet, wandering like her thoughts, had already carried her to the edge of Robin Hood's hollow. "I'm going to get Mother," she said to the oak, the songbirds in tree and sky, the outlaws.

She felt many eyes staring at her. Lionel, Rook, Rowan, the merry men, they all gawked.

It didn't matter. Mama would know what to do. Etty turned toward Fountain Dale.

Rowan limped forward to catch her by the arm. "Etty, wait."

"No. I'm going now."

"Lass, bide a bit." Robin Hood strode forward to stand in her way, reaching out toward her as if his touch could change her mind. "Wait and see whether your father's captain makes an offer."

"No." Wait and see, with Mother in that cage? Another minute would be too long. Etty stepped back from Robin. "I'm *going!*" Bleary-eyed from lack of sleep, she looked around, saw her bow and sheaf of arrows lying where she had dropped them, picked them up and slung them over her shoulder. She felt at the leather pouch on her belt; everything she needed was there. Her knife rode in its boarskin sheath. She was ready.

"Too risky," Rook growled.

Robin said, "He's right, lass. You can't."

"But I can and I will and I shall and I am going to." Feeling light-headed with relief, Etty grinned. "I'm the only one who can."

"Etty, sleep on it," Lionel put in.

When Mother had been sleeping in a cage for three days now? Were they insane?

"He's right." Rowan laid a quiet hand on Etty's arm. "You're too tired. You're not thinking clearly."

"I'm thinking like a jolly old logician!" Etty thought she was. Hands on her hips, she scowled at the group of them ranked between her and the edge of Robin's clearing. "Listen, idiots. You're all outlaws, with bounties on your heads. But I'm just a runaway. You can be killed. But there's no reward for anyone to kill me. As for capture, the man who wants to take me captive is *your* captive." She jabbed her forefinger toward her father's sullen form seated on the far side of the oak, out of earshot. "Without him, his men won't know what to do about me. At the very worst, if they detain me, I'll arrange an exchange of prisoners. I'm going." She brushed through them and through thornbushes into the forest. Only Lionel reached out to attempt to stop her.

"Only if I go with you," he said.

"*No*, curdlehead." She strode away.

Straight as an arrow's flight, and wishing she could be half as quick, Etty ran toward Fountain Dale. When she slowed, it was only to catch her breath, not for fear of guards. Let them threaten her all they liked.

But in fact, she encountered no guards. None.

Hot and panting from running, she paused, crouching, in the hazel bushes at the clearing's edge. "By Aristotle's beard," she murmured, scanning the clearing.

Throughout Fountain Dale, her father's men lolled in the sunshine, eating and talking, or sleeping on the sweet new grass. No guards stood around her mother's golden prison. However, sauntering from one group to another, a man-at-arms paused at the cage, lifting his mantle from his shoulders. "Whew, it's hot," he said in owlish tones. "My lady, do you mind if I lay this here for a moment?"

From her hiding place in the bushes, Etty heard her mother chuckle. "Thank you, good yeoman," said Mother's silver voice, "but I am quite warm now."

Etty edged sideward to look past him, and her eyes widened. In the cage, Elsinor of Auberon sat with mantle upon mantle wrapped around her, and blankets covering her feet.

"Some of the men lay their mantles under them to soften the ground," remarked the man-at-arms.

"Indeed, so they told me. And I must say, breakfast tastes much better when one is comfortably seated."

The man-at-arms peered at her owlishly. "And how was your dry crust of bread this morning, my lady?"

"Wondrous fine," she answered him just as soberly. "Somehow, miraculously, it had been transformed into hot sweet buns with slatherings of butter."

"Bother! Have the men been forgetting His Majesty's orders today? You'll vouch for me that it's not my fault?"

"A bit of wine," said Mother thoughtfully, "just a few sips to settle my stomach, would be lovely, and I'm not likely to remember anything about it at all."

"Did I hear a little bird sing of wine?" The man-at-arms gazed at the sky. "What a good idea." He strolled off, leaving his mantle lying on the floor of the cage.

Etty lunged up, burst out of the bushes and ran like a deer toward her mother.

Elsinor of Auberon sprang to her feet, scattering mantles and blankets. "Daughter!" she cried. "Oh, my darling!" She lunged to her knees at the edge of the cage, her bare arms reaching through the bars.

Etty spent only a moment in her mother's embrace. Tears stung her eyes, but she blinked them back; she had to be able to see what she was doing. "Wait just a minute, Mother," she whispered, and she tugged herself free, her rough fingertips snagging the linen of her mother's chemise.

"Ettarde, your hands!" Mother said with shock in her voice.

Darting to the cage door, Etty had to smile. Mother hadn't changed.

"I can't keep my hands soft and white in the forest, Mother," she called as she studied the large padlock that secured the cage.

"Truly?"

"Truly. Not if I want to eat."

"Well . . . have you at least been taking care of your teeth and hair?"

"Yes, Mother." Ettarde pulled from her pouch one of the strong steel bodkins she kept there. With a faraway look she probed the padlock.

"What's going on here?" said a man's gruff voice with phlegm in it; either he had a cold or he was getting old.

"Oh, Captain!" Mother sang in nightingale tones, as sweetly as if she were receiving visitors in the solarium at home. "How nice of you to come see me. You know my daughter, Princess Ettarde?"

"Pleased to meet you," Ettarde mumbled without looking up from the padlock she was picking. Mother was playing a desperate game, she knew, trying to get the captain to pretend with her that nothing untoward was happening. . . . Oh, blast. Out of the corner of her eye, Etty saw a second man join the first.

"And this is the sergeant of the men-at-arms, dear," Mother said.

"Delighted." Etty felt herself sweating. How long could Mother charm them into doing nothing? Confound the padlock, it was not cooperating. Etty thrust the bodkin into her belt and tried another one.

"Call your soldiers," said the gruff voice to someone. "Seize her."

"No, let her go." The new voice had to be the sergeant. "She'll lead us to the king."

"Is your head filled with fish guts? She has come for her mother. Why would they flee toward the king?"

A pox on everything, she had to get this padlock open now, quickly—

"*Mon foi*, shall I search for you the key, mademoiselle the princess?" asked an unexpected voice.

Etty jerked her head up, so startled she nearly dropped the bodkin. Then she blinked, startled anew, for right beside her stood a lovely white pony, saddled and bridled, its harness decked in crimson and yellow, with a yellow plume nodding between its ears. Beauregard, of course, held the reins, resplendent in his plumed hat once again, grinning wickedly in its shadow.

"You!" Etty gasped.

"*Probablement* it shall be in the breeches pocket in the pavilion," Beauregard continued.

Etty could not catch breath to answer. Her head spun, seeing him there, this boy who was supposed to be her accursed enemy, once again offering to befriend her. She couldn't think, let alone move, but she had to move, do things, free Mother. And it did not help her to see most of the men-at-arms gathered around as if for a cockfight, watching.

"I go search the key, *non*?" Beauregard offered.

"No," Etty whispered before she knew what she was saying. "No, stay here in case . . ." In case she needed him. She trusted him, blast it all, and she liked him. She had liked him from the first, and her heart had never led her wrong before. Was he really such a scoundrel as he seemed? Etty suspected not. Somehow that fake accent of his, and that devilish grin, calmed her fears. Things couldn't be too bad if Beauregard was still able to annoy her.

Just at that moment, things rapidly got worse. "Men," yelled the captain, "seize her!"

Etty gasped and took one last stab at the padlock, giving the bodkin a wild twist, and she felt the lock's iron innards give way at last. It fell open. She pulled it out of the latch. The cage door swung wide.

"No!" the sergeant yelled at the advancing soldiers. They hesitated, glancing at one another.

Barefoot, looking as fragile as frost in her chemise, Mother pattered forward to the door of her cage. "What a lovely pony," she told Beauregard.

"For you to ride, my lady." Beauregard swung the pony around for her to mount. "Her name, it is Dove."

"How sweet of you." The smile at the corners of Mother's eyes showed that she knew she was being absurd. But just the same, Mother would not give up her courtly courtesies unless blood started to flow. As seemed all too likely.

"*Seize* them!" the captain roared.

"No!" the sergeant shouted just as loudly. "Follow them."

The soldiers surged and muttered like waves of the sea, washing forward, then back. Beauregard grasped Queen Elsinor by the waist and set her upon the pony, lifting her easily although he stood no taller than she did. Etty grabbed the mantle lying at the edge of the cage and threw it around her mother's shoulders. Clicking his tongue, Beauregard tugged at the reins, urging Dove into a walk. Etty trotted to her mother's side.

A rough hand grasped her shoulder from behind.

Etty snatched her knife from her belt and struck. Whoever he was, he swore and jerked his hand away, but there were more captors now, more hands grabbing, clutching. Ettarde flailed with the knife, seeing no faces, only arms and grasping hands, a wall of men all around her.

Through the pounding panic in her ears she heard a hunter's horn blow three notes as soaring and joyous as the song of a lark. "Robin!" Etty cried.

There was a surge of sound, brush crackling, feet tramping. The soldiers around Etty froze. She dodged through them.

Ranged along the edge of the clearing stood two-score archers in Lincoln green, their six-foot yew bows drawn to the fullest, each with its clothyard shaft's honed-steel head pointed at a man-at-arms's chest. The men of Auberon outnumbered the outlaws three to one, but the soldiers weren't wearing their helms, most of them had laid aside the heavy quilted tabards they wore by way of breastplate, and some of them had even laid aside their weapons. They stood dumbstruck.

"Step back," commanded the tallest outlaw, Little John, and the soldiers did so.

From the forest strode a towering, brown-clad youth even taller than the outlaw captain. "Are you all right, my dear little lady?" he called.

All of Etty's fear melted into exasperation.

"Lionel—" The lummox, he could see she was fine. "I'm not your dear lady!"

Atop the white pony, her mother smiled at her over her shoulder. "Come, my dear little daughter," she called with a quirk of laughter in her silver voice. "We've tarried long enough. We really should be going."

Eleven

All right, Beauregard," said Robin, looking as vexed as Etty had ever seen him. "Explain."

"*Sacre bleu, mon ami,* what is there to explain? I go back to get Dove and my hat, that is all." Under the brim of that large plumed headgear, Beauregard rolled his sparkling dark eyes. "Why you shout at me? You think I leave Dove with those varlets who speak rudely to her and give her the forage fit only for cows?"

"Trickster knave—"

Etty burst out laughing. She couldn't help it. Imagine, Robin Hood calling someone else a trickster?

Robin scowled at her.

"Robin," Etty told him, laughing, "everything is all right. Let it go." The sun shone fairer than the king's gold, Mother sat on a throne of soft deerskins with worshipful outlaws clustered around her, Father had been banished into the giant oak tree's hollow trunk, and all was well compared with what it had been. Etty wanted only to enjoy the peace of the moment. "Judge a tree by its fruit, not by its leaves," she added.

"Euripides," Beauregard put in.

Etty gawked at him, but managed to continue her thought. "Beauregard helped me free my mother. And he came back here, didn't he?"

Robin said grimly, "What I need to know, first of all, is how he got away."

"*Mon foi*, why you not say so?" Beauregard could not have been more infuriating if he had thumbed his nose. "*C'est facile*. Easy. I climb inside the tree until I find a little hole, and out I slip, then away through the branches like a, how you call it, a squirrel." He flashed a grin.

Robin's eyes widened. "Lady have mercy."

"But I think the king Solon will not climb so, *non*?"

Once again Robin scowled. "Beauregard, I don't know what your game is—"

"Game? Why do you think I am playing a game?" Beauregard flared. By the way he squared his shoulders and dropped his Frankish accent, Etty could tell he meant it.

"You think I am a spy?" Beauregard challenged.

"I don't know what to think."

"Robin," Etty put in, "it's simple. Judge the tree—"

"I heard you the first time."

A gruff, unexpected voice spoke. "I was welcomed for less reason."

Several heads swiveled to stare at Rook, sitting there with his grimy hands on his scabby knees, his strand of the silver ring hanging by a thong on his bare chest.

"All I did was keep my mouth shut," he growled.

"You could have betrayed us," Rowan said, "but you did not." She turned to her father. "Just as Beauregard could have betrayed us—"

"And may yet do so!" Robin lifted his hands in appeal. "He comes here with bleached hair and a false accent and you want to trust him? We are *outlaws*! We cannot afford to let down our guard."

Although no one restrained him, Beauregard stood watching and listening, something impish dancing in his dark eyes.

Robin went on. "He's hiding something. Why would he wish to join us when he held a favored position at court? Why would he return here after I had imprisoned him? He *must* be a spy! There can be no other reason!"

Etty spoke up placidly. "But there *is* another reason, and I believe I know it."

Several heads turned toward her at once. Rowan

stared. Lionel peered. Robin frankly gawked. And Beauregard stood like a startled deer.

"Toads," Rowan murmured, peering at him, "you're pale. Are you all right?"

His dark eyes looked huge in his white face. He did not answer.

"There's no shame to your secret," Etty told him.

Still he did not speak, but just stood there poised as if to leap and flee.

Etty sighed and turned to Rowan. "Do you remember," she asked, "when I first met you, you were dressed as a boy, but I knew you were a girl?"

She heard someone gasp, perhaps Beauregard, and other voices murmuring, but she kept her eyes on Rowan, because it was always a treat to see Rowan smile.

Rowan did not fail her. She smiled like a summer day. "As I recall," she remarked, "you knew it because I showed such good sense."

"Is that what I said?"

"Yes, indeed it was." Rowan turned her smile on Beauregard, and Ettarde looked up to see that his fine-boned face had gone even paler than usual.

"In Rowan's case," Etty told him, "she had very few choices. She could serve the lord of a castle in all the ways such a lord usually uses a young woman, or she could wed some peasant for the sake of safety, or she could disguise herself as a boy and travel to Sherwood Forest to be with her father, Robin Hood."

Beauregard's eyes widened.

"You didn't know?" asked Ettarde wickedly.

"Etty, stop it," Rowan chided. "Don't torment him. Or her."

"You think he's a girl?" Robin demanded. "Why?"

"Because I've been using my brain, as someone once said I should." She gave him her most serene glance, reveling in the look on his face, as she went on. "Why would a page boy, a favorite of the high king, chuck it all to be an outlaw? I'll tell you why." Her voice softened. "Because soon her body will start to betray her. Already, maybe, she has to bind her chest. When her hips widen, or her voice fails to change, someone will guess."

She kept her eyes on Beauregard, but those dark eyes showed her nothing.

"And why would a page boy with a message follow a wayward king clear to Sherwood Forest?" she asked Robin.

It was a rhetorical question, and he did not answer it, but Lionel did. "Because he, I mean she, had heard about a certain runaway princess . . ."

"It's the only thing that makes sense," Etty said.

"Why stay away from the common latrines and the tents of the common soldiers? Why insist on staying in the most private—"

Lionel finished the thought. "In your father's pavilion, behind the draperies. When it must have taken a lot of insisting. Yes."

Ettarde added, "Sleeping fully clothed, with her boots on, just in case she had to flee."

Nodding, Rowan asked gently, "Beau?"

Silence, except for the forest sounds: breeze whispering in the budding branches, trickle of springwater somewhere under the loam, songbirds warbling, crooning, piping, and the cry of a falcon in the high sky. Ettarde studied Beau's face, as fair as a cameo, while Beau scanned each outlaw in turn. Finally Beau turned her gaze to Etty.

"How did you know?" she asked.

"You mean aside from logical thinking?" Etty shrugged. "Because you wear such exquisite clothes."

"*Mon foi*, that is one reason I left my people, because I wanted not to wear black and black and more black." Like a flower bursting into bloom from under a stone, Beau's irrepressible grin blossomed. She turned to Robin. "Which is worse, O Prince of Thieves, that I am of the accursed race or that I am a girl?"

Robin stared back at her, his eyes gray, cloudy—but

then it was as if the sun came out from behind the clouds. He smiled. "By my poor old bones, fooled by a girl again," he said as if being fooled were a great treat. "You'd think I would learn." His eyes shone, as blue as clear skies. "All right, Beau. Stay here with my welcome."

For once Beau did not give forth a flood of words. She just nodded.

"Judge a tree by its fruit, I have been told." Shaking his head, Robin turned to Etty. "Euripides," he added, round-eyed. "Good my young philosopher, what are we to do with your father?"

The question hit her like a cudgel, fit to knock her breath away. She sat speechless, for she knew all too well what she should do: go home to Auberon with her father and her mother, marry Lord Basil, prevent a war and save her father's kingdom. Surely this would be the noble course. Surely this was her duty as a princess, to save the common folk from suffering.

Surely she was a coward for not wanting to do it.

Yet what else *could* she do, now that she understood how peasants would cry and flee their burning huts and starve and die? What to do with her father, indeed? Kill him in cold blood?

Etty groaned and curled up to pillow her head on her knees.

"Lass, I forgot you've not slept. We can keep him another day." Robin sounded as gentle as a mother.

Mother.

She had not yet asked Mother what to do. And surely Mother would know. Ettarde lifted her head, stumbled to her weary feet, nodded to everyone and trudged off to seek Queen Elsinor.

Twelve

D earest, I wish you had never known of our problems at Auberon," said Ettarde's mother. "It is a hard choice your father has given you. You have been happy here?"

"Yes."

"I thought so. Such freedom. And how beautiful everything is!" Walking through Sherwood Forest with Etty, Mother gazed all around with shining eyes.

Etty blinked, looking anew at the satiny silver boles of beeches, the great oaks with their leaves just budding and the moss growing like green velvet on their northern sides. And mushrooms like great pearls pushing up through the loam, and the first violets just opening, while all around, the honey-golden notes of wrens and wood thrushes dripped down.

"Yes," she said, "it's lovely here. Mother, what *am* I to do?"

"I will not tell you what to do, darling."

"But—"

"I must not. You must decide. What if I tell you wrongly? You would grow to hate me."

"I could never hate you."

"Just the same, you are not a little girl anymore. I cannot tell you what you should do."

Etty's shoulders sagged as she walked on between the shadowy tree trunks. From every tree echoed the melodies of the birds. They sang so bravely, Etty knew, because it was their time to couple. Already some of them were building their nests. Why could it not be so sweet and simple for her?

Then Etty heard another silver thread of song, even sweeter:

> *"All you maidens, hear me sing,*
> *Let no man put you in a cage.*
> *Little songbirds, take to the wing*
> *and fly, fly away—"*

Etty turned to smile at her mother. "How did you know I was there," she asked, "the morning you sang that?"

Mother's tender mouth curved just a little at the corners. "Dearest, I sang it a hundred times a day."

They walked between looming oaks where jays scolded and rock doves cooed. Their path turned downward, into a green-shadowed ravine. Thrushes and wagtails and linnets and wrens sang of spring, love, eggs, nesting. Through their tapestry of song, Etty idly noticed the notes of a cuckoo.

"There are few enough choices for a woman," Mother said as if no silence had intervened in their conversation. "I never considered that I had any. I cannot make this choice for you, my daughter."

"Cuckoo," Etty murmured as the sleek gray voice kept calling. Outlaw bird that had no nest. "Backdoor bird." But where was the back door for her now?

At Etty's request, the four who wore the strands of the silver ring gathered in the rowan grove. Ettarde hoped that the ancient green magic of that place could somehow calm her and help her. And she hoped that the others could give her an answer. No, that was presuming too much, but she hoped that by voicing her thoughts to them, somehow she would find her way.

Sitting in a circle around the everlasting spring, they talked till twilight and got nowhere.

"Sleep on it, Etty," Rowan said at last, reaching out toward her.

"I can't sleep." Ettarde twisted her strand of the ring on her finger. "I ought to just give this back and go," she mumbled. "I am such a coward."

Lionel turned on her. "You're no coward! I'm the coward here, and I will allow no others."

"Oh, *certainly*."

"What have you done that entitles you to call yourself a coward?"

"I left Rowan in that man trap—"

"Very sensibly so," Rowan declared. "Moreover, that was last year. Each year we start anew. What have you done lately to claim cowardice?"

"Just kidnapped her father," Lionel grumbled, "and engaged him in scholarly debate, and rescued her mother from an armed camp, and stood up to Robin for Beauregard's sake."

Ettarde blinked, feeling a hazy revelation dawn: Perhaps there was some courage in her after all?

"Speaking of Beau," Rowan was saying, "she can't stay with Robin."

Lionel arched his owlish brows. "Don't you think Robin will come to accept her?"

"Yes, surely. I think he already has. But a girl among the merry men?" Rowan rolled her eyes in a rare show of impatience. "Have some sense. It would never have worked for me, and it won't work for her. Shall we take her into the band if she wishes it?"

In his usual gruff way, Rook spoke a single word. "Yes."

Lionel said, "I don't know. Not just because she's one of them, you know, the accursed race," he added hastily. "We're all outcasts here. But that blasted fake accent of hers drives me batty. You know she does it just to annoy."

Rowan smiled, agreeing. "She's worse than Robin."

"And not only that way. She's such a trickster, she may make an uncomfortable sort of comrade. I'm not sure of her yet."

Rowan nodded. "Etty?"

Worry and weariness had clotted Etty's mind until she felt as if her head were stuffed with nettles. Trying to think about Beauregard, she could summon no intelligence, only impressions and vignettes: Beau crying peevishly to the guards, "Radish-head, what you think? I sniff the night breezes, *non*?" Beau asking, "I search for you the key, *oui*?" Beau patting his white pony, then helping Mother onto the saddle. Beau flaring defiantly at Robin Hood, "The greatest thieves of all, are they not the kings and so-called lords of your race? My race holds no land, makes no wars, sheds no blood—"

Etty sat bolt upright, gasping, "That's it!"

"What?" Rowan and Lionel blurted together.

"That's *it!* Back door," explained Etty as lucidly as she was able. "I am an idiot." Greatly relieved, she lay down where she was and fell asleep within a moment.

She awoke at first light, her mind as clear and calm as the dawn. Quietly, trying not to disturb the others, she whispered an apology, as Rowan always did, to the spring, then dipped water. Usually she would have bathed in the stream that ran out of Fountain Dale, but now her father's soldiers camped there. Etty took her waxed leather buckets of water into the woods for privacy. Morning mist veiled her in white steam as she washed herself thoroughly with bear's-grease soap. She washed her hair, also, and checked it for nits, then combed it and braided it in a crown around her head. She cleaned her teeth, put on a fresh doeskin kirtle, and hung the dirty one over an oak limb to air. Songbirds were piping loud when she returned to the rowan grove, and the others were stirring.

"Rowan," Etty called softly, "I'm going to check on the state of things at Fountain Dale, then to speak with my father."

"Wait a bit and we'll come with you."

"I can't wait. I'll be all right." Walking away barefoot on the soft loam, with mist rising in ribbons all around her, Etty tucked the year's first violets into her hair.

There was a friendly panting sound, and fur tickled her leg. Tykell. His plumy tail waving in the air as he trotted beside her, he gave her a wolfish grin. She smiled back at him. Good. He could help her spy out the guards.

But treading softly to the verge of Fountain Dale, she found no guards. Although the sun was up now and had taken away the mist over the meadow, although a thousand birds were singing, Father's men still lay sleeping. Standing boldly behind the hazel bushes to survey the camp, Etty frowned in wonder. The tents had been knocked down, even her father's pavilion. It lay in a red-and-white mess on the ground. The men slept in the open on the grass, some at one end of the meadow and the rest at the other end. Halfway in between them, the cage had been battered into a pile of gold sticks. Clothing and cooking gear and oddments of harness lay strewn everywhere. Etty saw no bloody bodies, but even so, the place looked as she imagined the aftermath of battle.

Tykell lifted his head, looked over his thickly furred shoulder and gave a low woof, barely more than a grunt.

Etty turned just in time to see Robin Hood slip between young oaks to join her. And right behind him, almost as silently, walked Beau, hatless, a borrowed brown mantle hiding her vivid clothing and yellow hair.

"Well met, lass," Robin murmured to Etty.

She stood on tiptoe to kiss him on the cheek, then gave Beau an inquiring look. "Are you Robin's apprentice now? Following him?"

Beau gave her a devilish grin. "*Mais oui*, I am his apprentice in being an outlaw, and he is my apprentice in being a nuisance."

"Indeed she is," Robin agreed, a smile teasing at the corners of his mouth. "You came to see what your father's men might be doing, lass?"

"Yes," she said, matching his mock-sober tone, "to see whether they might be at the point of rescuing him anytime soon."

Robin's smile widened as he scanned the chaos in Fountain Dale, and his blue eyes glinted. "It would seem not."

In tones of utter disgust Beau put in, "The captain and the sergeant, they each have their followers; they have their own little war."

Etty gave her a curious look. On Beau's fair face she had seen a sneer similar to the one she had sometimes directed at the Wanderers. How odd, yet how very just, if the Wanderers scorned Ettarde's folk in like manner. "Do you despise us, Beau?"

"*War* I despise. So stupid."

Etty had been raised to consider war the proper and noble pursuit of well-born men. But look at Lionel, whose lordly father had tried to force him to be a warrior when all Lionel wanted was to play his harp. Imagine if the music had been beaten out of Lionel's hands by war's steely blows. And imagine what would happen to the folk of Auberon if Lord Basil made war upon the town.

Yes, war was fit to despise. Etty nodded.

"But despise you, no. I like not to despise people."

Beau had an accent of her own, Etty noticed, when she was not being Frankish. Maybe the fake Frankish accent had been to cover up her real one in the king's court. Or maybe . . . maybe it was Beau's way of covering up other aspects of herself. Feelings, perhaps?

Beau's brilliant grin softened to a smile. "Wanderers despise folk who stay in one place like toadstools—but I have left my people. I try to despise no one."

Somebody at Fountain Dale blew a few sleepy notes on a horn, signaling sleepers to awaken. It was time to disappear. Etty turned and slipped into the forest. The sun had not yet cleared away the mist there; it still swirled in white tendrils around Etty's bare ankles. The others followed her as she picked her way up a steep rise amid ferns and bracken, under forest shade draped with grape and ivy, bound toward Robin Hood's oak.

She needed to have one more talk—she hoped it would be just a talk—with her father.

Thirteen

S he wanted to speak with her mother privately first,
but there was no chance. Her father spotted her the
moment she stepped into the clearing. There under the
giant oak he sat, clothed in the borrowed jerkin and
leggings of a common yeoman but as imperious as ever,
despite being flanked by outlaw guards.

"Daughter!" he roared across the shady hollow at Ettarde. "Have you yet seen your clear duty? Might we
depart from this accursed wilderness?"

Her father's shouting still made her tremble. But she
kept that reaction to herself, forcing herself to reply in
tones that were quick, loud and cheery, like the song of
a mistle thrush. "You may go when you like, Father.
Where's Mother?"

"Here!" came a silvery call, and her mother hurried
toward her from the other side of the oak, still barefoot

and in her chemise, but with an outlaw's cloak wrapped around her for warmth. Etty hugged her and felt her mother's embrace like a blessing. Many times in the past day she and her mother had embraced, but still not enough.

Father bellowed, "What mean you, daughter? Approach me!"

Ettarde gave him a blank stare and sat down where she was, near the cooking fire. Mother sat also, across from Ettarde, at the farthest possible point from King Solon. At the edges of her attention, Ettarde was aware of Beau and Robin standing by, listening, and other outlaws going about their business in silence unusual for them.

Ettarde helped herself to one of the scones that lay near the fire to warm. She took a big bite of the warm bread and chewed it well before she told the king, "What I mean, Father, is that you may go where you will when you will, and I will stay here."

"What!" His glare seemed to pierce Etty like a sword, as always, and he seemed huge to her, his wrath swelling him like a toad. But she kept herself from shrinking back as he ranted at her. "What impudence is this? Thoughtless wench, do you care nothing for the brave men who will perish unless you—"

"But the folk of Auberon are your subjects, Father,

not mine." Etty made sure to speak clearly and calmly. "And the fault will be yours, not mine, if they die."

It was as if she had thrown cool water into hot oil. Her father sputtered, his temper in such a boil that he could barely speak. He could only flare, "Impudent hussy—"

"It is up to you, Father. And peace is within your power. No lives need be lost." She spoke slowly, each word a chessman to be moved so that maybe her father would notice, would hear her—or so Ettarde hoped, although in her heart she knew better. "All you need to do is leave the gates of Auberon open for Lord Basil. Let him in. Give the holding over to him."

In the instant of silence that followed, Etty tried to sit solid like a rock and not cringe. Keeping her eyes on her father as he gawked, still she felt Robin's stare, her mother's wondering glance. She heard a cuckoo singing and knew that most folk would think her crazy. She felt Beau's eyes upon her and wondered if the stranger girl knew it was from her, Beauregard du Fleur Noir, that Ettarde had learned this back door: War was not a necessity, but a choice men made. King Solon the Red could save his own people if he really wanted to.

She braced herself for his response.

He seemed to struggle for breath at first. Then he burst into abuse. "Fool! Simpleton! Lackwit girl! Can such a goose girl be a daughter of mine? Senseless—"

Etty remarked, " 'When you have no basis for an argument, abuse the plaintiff.' Cicero."

"Argument?" roared King Solon. "Argument? There can be no argument! The kingdom of Auberon is my right, my inheritance, my destiny! I—"

" 'Are you not ashamed of heaping up the greatest amount of money and honor and reputation,' " quoted Ettarde, " 'and caring so little about wisdom and truth and the greatest improvement of the soul?' Socrates." Growing aware of sparrows chuckling in the spreading oak overhead, of smiles spreading among the listeners, Etty kept her face under control and her eyes steadily upon her father.

"I was a fool," he said grimly, "a wrongheaded fool to forget the right order of things, to let you learn from books."

"Not so, Father. I thank you for teaching me." Ettarde leaned toward him, for she really wanted him to understand. "You are a very good scholar." She paused, bracing herself to say what was next in her thoughts. "But Father, you are not a good king."

"And not a good husband," said a quiet, sweet voice Etty had not expected. Her mother.

King Solon felt that voice, Etty saw. It struck him

speechless. But he lifted his chin, his pointed beard, like a weapon.

Etty said earnestly, "Father, your kingdom is an accident of your birth, that is all. Think! Has it not always been a burden to you, making you harsh and bitter?" For a rueful moment Etty wondered what her father would have been like had fate not made him a king. Whether he would have treated her with more of a father's love. But it was no use thinking of what might have been. "Has not your truest heart been always with your books? Why not cast off the cares of Auberon, join a monastery—"

"Bah! You're insane," he said hoarsely. As if her words frightened him, with much haste but small dignity he scrambled to his feet.

From off to one side an utterly unexpected voice said, "'There is no genius free from some tincture of madness.' Seneca." It was Beau who spoke.

"*Mon foi!*" Ettarde exclaimed, grinning at her.

"Impudence beyond impudence," stormed King Solon as he thrust a shaking finger at Ettarde. "You— vixen, wretched shrew—you no longer deserve to be called my daughter."

She turned back to him, sober again. "I am sorry you feel that way, Father."

This was true. With a pang in her heart she wished it were otherwise between them.

Does he love me, deep inside? At all?

Likely she would never know.

King Solon ranted, "Bah! A pox on you and all your cohorts. Stay here and bear my curse."

"If the innocent folk of Auberon bleed and die, Father," Etty told him quietly, "it will not be by my doing."

"Idiocy!" He turned to storm away, but the guards seized him by the arms. "Unhand me!" he shouted, struggling against them no more effectively than a bug. The guards looked to Robin, and Robin looked to Etty.

"Let him go back to Fountain Dale," she said.

Robin told the guards, "Guide him there."

Take him by a long and roundabout path, he meant. They started to blindfold the king first, so that he would not learn the way to Robin's hideout. But King Solon ducked the strip of cloth, looked over his shoulder and snapped at his wife, "Come, woman!"

Queen Elsinor remained seated by the fire, shaking her head serenely. "I will visit with my daughter yet awhile, good my lord."

"I bade you come!"

She did not move, but said as pleasantly as if she spoke of the weather, "What, after you put me in a cage? I cherish and obey you no longer, my lord. Go your ways."

The guards blindfolded him and tugged him toward the forest. "My curse on all of you!" he screamed as they half carried him away.

Several days later, footsore and much farther north, Etty stood at the edge of a forest called Barnesdale Wood, gazing over common land where the prickles of last year's furze were being burned to make way for new green shoots. Peering beyond smoke and small flame, Ettarde could see soft hills, a lazy loop of river, freshly plowed strips of field, and then the village and the fortress of Celydon.

"I never thought to come home to my brother as such a beggar," murmured her mother from atop the white pony, Dove.

Etty placed her hand on Dove's swanlike neck and looked up at her mother with a smile. Mother, who had no shoes, rode the elegant pony. The rest of them had walked: Beau, Lionel, Rowan, Rook, Ettarde herself, and a few of Robin Hood's men for an added measure of safety. They had been walking since the hour Ettarde had sent King Solon on his way. Etty had decided then, with her mother's agreement and Robin Hood's blessing, that it was better for her and her mother to be elsewhere in case King Solon managed to rally his men-at-arms and attempt to reclaim his wife and daughter.

Etty had run to the rowan hollow first, to say good-bye to Rowan and Lionel and Rook, but the band had refused to be left behind. Now here they all stood at the outskirts of Celydon Manor.

And Ettarde had to make yet another hard decision.

Between what she wanted and what she knew she had to do.

But there was no choice, really. Ettarde looked down at her own hands, her knuckles rough and her nails ragged from shelling hazelnuts and shooting arrows and digging wild parsnips and gathering firewood and playing at quarterstaffs with Rowan. Uncle Marcus would not approve of her hands any more than Mother did. Slowly, careful not to sigh, Etty slipped the thin silver ring off her finger.

"Not for my sake, please, dear," said her mother's soft voice, like an angel's, from above.

Etty shook her head. "No." Although in truth she was thinking partly of her mother, whose life had taken some hard turns of late. Etty considered that Mother deserved to have her daughter by her side when she entered Celydon castle to ask her brother, the lord, for aid and shelter. But Etty's greater concern was for Rowan and Lionel and Rook and, yes, Beau. And Robin

Hood. Ettarde knew quite well that, until she learned her father's intentions, she must consider herself a danger to the others in her band and all the outlaws in the forest. Let Uncle Marcus bear the task of protecting her and dealing with Solon the Red.

Etty knew what she had to do. Still, she could not quite help blinking back tears as she turned to Rowan and held out her strand of the silver ring.

There was a murmur of dismay from the others. Rowan took a step back, exclaiming, "No, Etty, keep it."

"But I want you to have it. Or give it to Beau." Etty turned to the proud, dark-eyed girl, who wore brown leggings and a brown mantle with her crimson tunic now. "Let her take my place."

Rowan said, "No one can take your place. We'll welcome Beau for her own sake . . . " Rowan shot a questioning glance at Lionel. With only a single, appealing glance heavenward, he nodded. Rowan nodded back. "We'll welcome Beau for her own sake if she wants to stay." And Rowan, also, turned gravely to Beau.

Overhead, the little brown tree-creeper birds twittered and drummed, but for once Beau seemed at a loss for words. Her mouth softened like a shy child's, her eloquent eyes widened, and in their gaze Ettarde sensed a muddle of surprised emotion: joy, fear, doubt, longing. In that moment, Ettarde felt that Beau could have been her sister. She blurted, "Beau, your parents, your people—why did you run away?"

The girl fixed her with her midnight gaze. "Because they beat me," she said. "Always beat, beat, beat. To make me be silent and maidenly."

Lionel chuckled. "You? Silent?"

Her sudden grin flashed. "You see! It is useless, *non*?"

"No. I mean, yes."

Rowan pulled from her finger the three remaining strands of the puzzle ring that had been her mother's, and separated one. "For Beau," she said, offering it. "We are an outlaw band, Beau, and you will be a strand of the band. Without being silent and maidenly."

The outcast girl took it, saying nothing. Perhaps she could not speak. Etty noticed that her dark eyes swam liquid, like wells.

"Etty, keep yours," Rowan said. "You will always be one of us."

"I will try—" Etty heard her voice wavering, steadied it and started over. "I will try to come back to you."

They all stood looking at each other, but that could not go on forever. It was time. Etty turned to give her mother a hand, and Queen Elsinor began to dismount.

"No! No, keep the little Dove, take her with you," Beau said all in a breath.

Etty turned to her in astonishment. She knew how Beau adored Dove. "But she's yours!"

"Not so." Impish thoughts glinted in Beau's eyes. "She belongs to the stables of the high king."

Lionel complained, "Porridgehead, you're an outlaw now! You're dead if the king catches you."

"True. But there is scant forage for a pony in the wildwood," Beau said. "Take her." Beau's eyes flashed up to Queen Elsinor's pale face. "Good my lady, ride her into Celydon, do, and no one will call you a beggar."

So that was it.

A royal gift, and Etty knew she had to swallow her pride and accept it. She gave the dark-eyed girl the nod of an equal. "Thank you."

Her mother echoed her words. "Beau, thank you."

"No, my lady, no, Princess Ettarde, thank *you*."

Etty hugged Beau—finally it felt right to touch and hug this oddling. Then she put her arms around Rook, who stank—a pox on it; Etty hugged the wild boy anyway. And big, gentle Lionel got a long hug. And finally Rowan. Rowan Hood, mystic and healer, the one to whom they all looked as leader, although she considered herself their equal—Rowan was the hardest one to leave. Etty gave her a fierce embrace and turned away quickly.

There. Celydon. Maidservants, baths, proper meals, rich gowns to wear—how miserable. Blinking, Etty laid a hand on Dove's neck, looked up at her mother's pale face, nodded and walked out of the forest.

Rowan's voice sounded behind her, grave and steady, as always. "Come back if you need us."

And Lionel called, his voice not nearly as steady, "You know your way. If you need us . . . my dear little lady."

Etty grinned, and knew she should tell him she was not his dear little lady, but she could not speak. She could barely see her way, what with tears stinging and blurring her eyes. She did not dare look back at her friends lest she break down altogether. But she lifted a hand to show that she had heard them, and leading her mother's white pony, Princess Ettarde strode across sheep pasture toward Celydon.

" 'Nothing lasts forever except change,' " Beau called to her from the forest she was leaving behind. "Hera-clitus."

Confound the rascal. Etty smiled.